ZOM-B FUGITIVE

DARREN SHAN

SIMON AND SCHUSTER

First published in Great Britain in 2015 by Simon and Schuster UK Ltd
A CBS COMPANY

1 3 5 7 9 10 8 6 4 2

Simon & Schuster UK Ltd
1st Floor
222 Gray's Inn Road
London WC1X 8HB

www.simonandschuster.co.uk

Simon & Schuster Australia, Sydney
Simon & Schuster India, New Delhi

A CIP catalogue record for this book
is available from the British Library.

HB ISBN: 978-0-85707-792-9
TPB ISBN: 978-0-85707-793-6
EBOOK ISBN: 978-0-85707-795-0

Printed and bound by CPI Group (UK) Ltd, Croydon, CR0 4YY

MIX
Paper from
responsible sources
FSC
www.fsc.org   FSC® C020471

Simon & Schuster UK Ltd are committed to sourcing paper that
is made from wood grown in sustainable forests and supports the Forest
Stewardship Council, the leading international forest certification organisation.
Our books displaying the FSC logo are printed on FSC certified paper.

OBE (Order of the Bloody Entrails) to:
Lorraine Keating – looking good in the hat!

Editorial Fugitives:
Elv Moody
Emma Young
Kate Sullivan
Leslie Shumate

Fellow Fugitives on the Chain Gang:
the Christopher Little Agency

THEN . . .

Becky Smith's journey into darkness and pain began when a zombie ripped her heart from her chest and she became one of the walking, brain-eating undead.

Months later she recovered consciousness. As a child, she had been injected with a vaccine by someone working for a century-old scientist called Dr Oystein, and that had bestowed her with the ability to regain her senses.

After a spell of captivity in an underground complex, B was set free by the nightmarish Mr Dowling, a mad, vicious clown who was backed by an army of mutants. He killed gleefully wherever he went, but for some reason he let B walk away unharmed.

B found her way to Dr Oystein's base in County

Hall, where she became one of his Angels, a team of revitalised, teenage zombies. The doctor had been forced by the Nazis to create the zombie virus, and he believed he was on a mission from God to make amends and help mankind overcome this most hideous of threats.

The doctor told B that he had subsequently created another pair of viruses which were the key to the outcome of the war between the living and the undead. One was a dark red liquid called Clements-13, which would wipe out every zombie on the face of the planet within a couple of weeks if released. The other was Schlesinger-10, a milky-white substance which would have an equally fast, fatal impact on humans if it was uncorked.

Dr Oystein couldn't use Clements-13 to eliminate the undead forces because Mr Dowling had stolen a vial of Schlesinger-10 from his laboratory, with the help of his ally, the mysterious Owl Man. The clown could unleash the virus on humanity if the doctor forced his hand, just as Dr Oystein could crack open his vial of Clements-13 if Mr Dowling ever attacked him. The pair were locked in a stalemate and the world looked like it would suffer indefinitely because of it.

The Angels did whatever they could to help the survivors of the zombie apocalypse, but their ultimate goal was to track down Mr Dowling's supply of Schlesinger-10. If they retrieved the vial from the killer clown, Dr Oystein could bring his sample of Clements-13 into play and deliver the world from its undead menace in one fell swoop.

When B was captured by a hunter called Barnes, an ex-soldier from America who was an expert when it came to killing or capturing zombies, destiny set her on course for a showdown with Mr Dowling. Barnes was working for the Board, a group of rich and powerful humans who had granted his son a place on an island where zombies couldn't attack him. In return for this favour, Barnes was obliged to hand B over to the Board, whose members gleefully passed the time by watching her duel to the death with other zombies.

A repentant Barnes later helped B escape, before

setting off to rescue his son, whose safety was no longer guaranteed now that his father had betrayed his foul employers. But B wasn't finished with the Board, and again ended up in their clutches months later. The most twisted of their party was the fiendish Dan-Dan, who strapped her down in his quarters in Battersea Power Station, and proceeded to pick her body apart as painfully as he could.

It looked as if B's time was up, but, to her shock, Mr Dowling charged to her rescue. Aided by his mutants and a team of lethal, genderless babies, he swarmed the Power Station and freed her.

The clown's babies carried B deep underground to Mr Dowling's lair, where he patched her fragile carcass back together. She found out that the babies had been cloned from her DNA, making her their virtual mother. The clown wanted her to marry him and rule by his side, so that they could eventually replace humanity with their eerie offspring.

B wasn't interested in playing happy families with Mr Dowling, but, as he shared his memories with her, she began to feel sorry for him. He had been a decent man once, until something dreadful happened and cast him into a state of insane chaos.

When Mr Dowling promised to stop killing if B married him, she bowed to his wishes, hoping it might signal the start of his recovery. After a warped but oddly sweet ceremony, the pair retired to their wedding chamber, where the clown granted her access to his innermost thoughts.

It should have been a peaceful, loving time, but B found herself instinctively smashing through Mr Dowling's mental defences. Without having planned it, she pinpointed the location of his vial of Schlesinger-10. The betrayed clown tried to kill her and the pair fought fiercely. B got the better of her husband, but, before she could finish him off, the enraged babies stormed the room and ripped into her. They would have killed her, but one of their own – Holy Moly, a baby with a hole in its head – reminded them that B was their mummy. Confused, they let her go, and she set off through the underground lair, wounded and alone, in search of the vial which would ensure victory for mankind if she could deliver it safely into the hands of Dr Oystein, but all too aware that time was against her and that Mr Dowling and his mutants would surely execute her if they caught up.

NOW ...

ONE

I left Mr Dowling unconscious. I zapped him with enough electricity to put a normal person out of action for a whole day. But the clown is far from normal and I can't bank on him staying down for too long. I reckon I might have as little as an hour or two before he stirs and calls for help. Maybe less if Kinslow or one of his other mutants comes to check on him. Time, as they say, is of the essence.

The trouble is, the shape I'm in at the moment, I'd struggle to win a race with a snail. Although Mr Dowling repaired the worst of the damage, I hadn't fully recovered from Dan-Dan's mauling by the time of my wedding. The babies reopened lots of old wounds when they attacked me, and inflicted plenty of new ones.

Every step is agony. The recently restored flesh of my stomach has been clawed away. Most of my replacement ribs have been snapped off. Bones are broken. I'm bleeding all over, thick, gloopy blood slowly oozing from my injuries. I didn't think there was that much of the crimson stuff left – Dan-Dan drained off lots of it while he was torturing me – but there must have been hidden reserves.

I'll have to do something about the blood. The loss won't really harm me, but if I don't stop it, I'll leave a trail that even a blind mutant will be able to follow. Still, I can't worry about that until I locate the vial of Schlesinger-10. If Mr Dowling recovers sooner than I anticipate, he'll know exactly where I'm going and he'll set the mutants on me. No point wasting time. My priority has to be to lay my hands on the vial. Only then can I start planning my next move.

I stagger along, picking my way from room to room through the maze which Mr Dowling and his assistants have built over the years. If this wasn't the day of my wedding, there'd be mutants relaxing, working and patrolling the corridors, even this far from the centre of the complex. But the celebrations must still be going strong, because I encounter no one. They're all toasting my health in the wedding chamber, unaware that their master is lying on his honeymoon bed unconscious, while their newly crowned mistress is plotting their downfall.

I'd love to return to Mr Dowling's bedroom-cum-laboratory and immerse myself in the pool of restorative blood and brains. A long soak in that would cure many of my ills. With all the mutants still celebrating the wedding, there's a chance I could steal in, rest up, then slip out again without anyone spotting me. But it's too risky — if one of them spots me in my bloody, bedraggled state, they'll know something is up and raise the alarm.

I don't even stop for a few minutes to rest, since the clock is ticking. Instead I push myself as hard as

I can, ignoring the agonised protests of my body as I force it through the pain barrier once again.

I come to a room that looks the same as the others. I would have passed through at any other time and thought nothing of it. But I know from Mr Dowling's stolen memories that there's a hidden door here, so I stop, treat myself to a short pause, then go looking for it.

I shuffle to the wall on my right and lift down the upper half of a woman's carcass from where it hangs on a hook. The wall behind her is caked with dried blood and dung. The babies bit off some of my artificial finger bones, but several remain intact. I use them to chip away at the mess. After a while, it starts to fall off in chunks and the outline of a door is revealed.

There's a small, old-fashioned combination lock in the centre, the type where you roll the tumblers one at a time until they click into place. I prised the numbers from Mr Dowling's memory and they're somehow still clear in my mind — it's like I have perfect recall. I start entering the digits until they read

528614592. Then I push down on the slim handle and the door opens.

I stare suspiciously into the gloom of the tunnel on the other side. I still don't know how I wrung so much information out of Mr Dowling. I hadn't planned to squeeze his secrets from him. I didn't think that I could. Something happened in the bridal suite that I had no control over, and it unnerved me. I don't like the fact that I operated on auto-pilot like a cold, calculating, experienced spy.

But what are my options? I can't go back. Mr Dowling will slaughter me on sight if I don't get out of here. I might be his beloved, but he can't let me live, knowing what I know. I've got to press ahead as fast as I can. It doesn't matter how I came by this knowledge. I need to cash in on it, and quickly, before the mutants lock down the complex and come hunting for me.

I enter the tunnel and push the door closed behind me — there's no way of operating the lock from this side, so I just have to hope that Mr Dowling's mutants don't spot the disturbance and investigate.

Then I press on through the gloom. This area isn't brightly lit, just the occasional light. But that's OK. I know the way. I could find it blindfolded if I had to.

The tunnel forks and I take the left turn. Then a right, another right, a left. These tunnels are roughly carved. Mr Dowling only used a few of his mutants when creating them, in secret, away from the gaze of his other followers. All of the workers were killed once they'd finished, like the slaves who built the tombs for the pharaohs in ancient Egypt. He didn't want anyone to know about this hidden network. It was created for his personal use only.

More twists and turns. I take them without thinking, following the map which was clear as crystal inside Mr Dowling's brain. He often comes here to check on his deadly prize, standing before it in ecstatic but horrified awe, like a worshipper at the shrine of some all-destructive god. There are several entrances and routes. He tests them all out on a regular basis, making sure the doors work, that the paths are clear of cave-ins, that no one has been sniffing around his toxic treasure.

It's not a long journey but I make poor time. I'm incapable of rushing. Still, as slow as I am, I'm dogged, and eventually I draw to a halt at another locked door. This one is protected by four combination locks, each requiring a twelve-digit code, and you'd need a serious stash of dynamite to make an impression on the door or wall. It would take a crack team a lot of time and hassle to break through. Even Ivor Bolton, an Angel who can open almost any lock, would have to admit defeat if confronted with these devilish beauties.

But I have the inside scoop, the elaborate string of numbers flashing in my mind's eye as if highlighted on a neon billboard. I start spinning the tumblers and soon I've set all forty-eight windows correctly. I grasp the round handle and twist. There's a sighing sound and the door opens inwards, widening the more I turn the handle, like a giant opening its mouth.

I step into a small, steel-lined room. There's a single light hanging from the centre of the ceiling. It switched on automatically as the door opened.

17

A safe sits in the middle of the room, bolted to the floor. The code for this lock is simpler than any of the others. Mr Dowling figured that if someone made it this far, the game was up. He set the code out of a sense of irony more than anything else, aware of the things that Dr Oystein has said about him over the years. I chuckle weakly as I spin the tumblers to the most diabolical of numbers — 666.

The safe opens and I sink to my knees. I reach in and pull out a clear tube, no more than twenty centimetres long. It's sealed with what looks like a plain rubber cork, but I know the cork is made from a special material and is absolutely airtight. It will never shrink or shake loose. And, although the tube appears to be just glass, again it's been carefully manufactured from a far tougher substance. You could put it on the floor and whack it with a sledgehammer, over and over, without even cracking it.

Just to be safe, there's a second clear, corked tube nestled within the first, every bit as indestructible as the outer container. And then, snuggled within that, is a vial, maybe fifteen centimetres long, filled with a milky-white liquid. There's no label on any of the containers, but I don't need one.

'*Schlesinger-10*,' I croak, holding the tube up to the light, watching the liquid as it splashes around inside the vial.

I never wondered what it would be like to hold the lives of every living human in your hands. Now that I'm in that position, I find it absolutely terrifying. I know I can't do any damage to the tubes. I'd have to deliberately uncork the first, slide out the second, uncork that, then slip out and uncork the vial in order to unleash the hounds of havoc. But I still feel sick at the nightmarish thought of the tube slipping through my fingers and somehow smashing open. I guess it's like doing a bungee jump — you know you're safely attached, but try telling that to your natural instincts when you're about to hurl yourself off the side of a cliff.

Reverently, knowing I'm not worthy of such a grave responsibility, I lower the tube and look for a place to store it. But there are no pockets in my

wedding dress. I could carry it but I want both hands free. So where . . . ?

With a grisly snicker, I stick the tube inside my stomach and root around until I find some pliant flesh to wedge it into. I grit my teeth as I work the tube firmly into place, taking no chances, not worrying about the discomfort. When I'm satisfied, I shake myself roughly and jump up and down. The brief burst of exercise almost makes me faint, but the tube doesn't budge. It's secure.

I feel like an expectant mother, only, instead of carrying a baby, I'm carrying hope for the entire world. If I can get this to Dr Oystein, the stalemate will be broken and he can release a sample of Clements-13, bringing the curtains crashing down on every zombie and mutant on the face of the planet.

'So, no pressure,' I giggle.

Then I put all humorous thoughts aside, turn my back on the safe, limp into the corridor and make my slow, sluggish, excruciating break for freedom.

TWO

Although most of the access points to the secret tunnels are situated in Mr Dowling's base, a few open out into the area beyond. He wanted to be able to skirt the main complex in case it ever fell into the hands of his enemies. As crazy as he is, he likes to cover as many angles as possible.

I absorbed all sorts of memories from the clown, more than I realised at the time. I knew that I was confirming the location of his vial of Schlesinger-10, but I also tapped into recollections of countless trips that he's made through his underground domain. My mind's full of maps and ways out of here.

Assessing that information, I try to come to a decision — should I head straight for the surface or stick to the shadows for a while?

The nearest exit is through Whitechapel Station. It wouldn't take me long to reach it, even in my current shuffling state. I could climb up through the station and lose myself on the streets.

Whitechapel would be my first preference, except I know from Mr Dowling's memories that the station is always carefully guarded by his forces, along with the one at Aldgate East. The guards might have been pulled from their posts to attend the wedding, but I can't count on that. It's unlikely that the mutants would have left themselves completely open to a sneak attack.

The alternative is to make use of the various tunnels and link up with the Tube line further west, pop up out of a random station. In its favour — the mutants can't patrol every stretch of tunnel, and they won't know which area of the city to focus their

search on once they discover I'm missing. Against —
I'll have to spend a lot of time in darkness, meaning
I might not see them coming if they happen to
chance upon me, and it will be hard, probably
impossible, to outrun them if they stumble across my
trail before I make it to the streets.

I spend a couple of minutes weighing up the pros
and cons, figuring it's time worth investing. In the
end I decide I'd be safer in the dark. I don't like it
down here, but just as it would be hard for me to see
any hunters coming, it would be equally difficult for
them to spot me going.

Having made up my mind, I first head in the
direction of Whitechapel. I'm aware that I've left a
trail of blood, and I'm hoping to throw off my track-
ers by continuing east for a spell, to make them think
that I'm aiming for the easiest way out. I'm probably
being naive – chances are they have mutants who've
been trained to detect the subtlest of scents – but I've
nothing to lose by trying.

After several minutes, I stop in the glow of a light
and start ripping the remains of the lower lengths of

my wedding dress into strips. It was such a lovely dress, and I hate having to wreck it, but it was already in tatters after the attack by the babies. The veil is missing, huge holes have been torn or bitten out of the material, its colour is now more crimson than white in most places.

I ball up some of the strips and press them deep into my flesh where I'm bleeding worst, plugging the gashes, stemming the flow as best I can. I wince as the material bonds with my flesh, sticking to it like an extra layer. As the balls absorb my blood and swell within me like flowers in bloom, I loop more of the makeshift bandages round my feet and ankles so that they'll hopefully soak up the drops trickling down my legs.

I study myself when I'm done. Far from perfect – I'd never have made a nurse – but it will have to do. The most important thing is that the vial has remained steady within its nesting place. My movements haven't shaken it loose by even a fraction. That's good to know going forward, means I don't have to stop to check on it too often.

I listen intently for a minute, trying to detect whether the hunters are already on my trail. I hear shuffling sounds close by and stiffen, thinking my number is up. But then I spot a couple of rats gnawing on an old bone and I relax. I suppose I should be grateful that the rodents don't attack me — I'd make a tasty snack for a big enough group of them. If I was human, they'd probably take me down, wounded and bleeding as I am, but zombie blood must not appeal to them.

When I'm sure that there are no mutants lurking nearby, waiting to spring upon me the second I turn my back, I take a deep breath – pointless since I don't have any lungs, but it's a force of habit – swing a left and arc back upon myself, heading west, deeper into the twisting network of tunnels.

THREE

After a while, I move out of the system of secret tunnels into old, disused sewers, the walls crumbling, the floors long dried up, relics of the past, forgotten by all except the mutants who discovered them when scouting around to find the perfect location for their base. Judging by the complete silence, I think even the rats and insects of London don't know about these ancient arteries.

It's pitch-black here and I have to feel my way along. There's no way up to the streets from these abandoned sewers – at least none that Mr Dowling is aware of – but they link with the Tube lines in several places, offering me a choice of exits when I've advanced further.

I think a normal, living person would be afraid if they found themselves in my position. The isolated sewers have a ghostly feel to them, and it's easy to imagine the spirits of the past drifting around me as I stumble ahead, or monsters like the Minotaur roaming freely, looking for victims.

But, seeing as how I'm an undead monster myself, I have nothing to fear. In fact, despite my earlier misgivings, I'm starting to feel at home — in the ragged remains of my torn, bloodstained white dress, with all my injuries and disfigurements, I could easily pass for an otherworldly spectre. If I didn't have a priceless cargo to deliver, this would be a good place to rest up, wait for my senses to dissolve, then crash around in for the next few thousand years. I couldn't do any harm down here, lost to the world of the conscious, out of sight and out of mind.

As I'm edging forward blindly, thinking about maybe coming back here if I manage to complete my mission, I hear noises from far off. At least I think they're far away, but it's hard to be certain in this sub-terranean realm, where the tunnels do strange things to sounds. Sometimes an echo carries for hundreds of metres, through a series of corridors, strong and vibrant. Other times a loud bang can be smothered by the hungry walls before it leaves a room.

I can't tell for sure whether the noises came from a near or distant source, but I know that they're voices. *Angry* voices.

I pause and listen cautiously, but the voices fade away a few seconds later, plunging me back into silence. I could wait for the sounds to come again, but that would be suicidal. I know what the voices mean. The alarm has been raised. The mutants are coming after me.

The chase is on.

FOUR

I'd like to push the pace – I'm conscious all the time of the precious vial nestled inside me, and the need to get it to Dr Oystein as quickly as I can – but I can't go any faster. I'm too injured, too exhausted. Besides, I'm better off taking my time. Even if I was at my physical peak, I probably wouldn't risk proceeding at more than a crawl. In the darkness, with all manner of unseen obstacles to contend with, I'd be tripping over with every few rushed steps. Slowly does it, girl.

Voices carry to me every so often, shouts, grunts, hisses. But there are never faces to go with the voices.

The mutants don't cut across my trail, and I continue to huff and puff along in the dark.

Until suddenly I spot the light of a torch coming towards me. By the glow, I see that I'm in a long tunnel, one of the old, decrepit sections of the sewers. The light is coming from a smaller, more recently constructed tunnel, ahead and to my left. I freeze and look for a hiding place, but there are no niches that I can duck into, no piles of debris to hide behind.

Fear lends me an unexpected burst of energy and I hurry to the opening of the side tunnel. As the person holding the torch draws close, I press myself against the wall, trying to disappear into the shadows, hoping I won't be noticed if the mutant – it has to be one of Mr Dowling's team, it couldn't possibly be anyone else – focuses their attention dead ahead, where the beam is brightest.

Two mutants step out into my stretch of tunnel. The one holding the torch is a tall guy, his face covered in the scabs and sores common to his kind. He sweeps the beam left then right. I'm almost directly behind him. For once I'm delighted that I don't have lungs. It means I don't have to hold my breath.

'This is ridiculous,' the shorter mutant snorts. 'We're never going to find her. It's like –'

'If you say "looking for a needle in a haystack" again, Glenn, I'll throttle you,' the mutant with the torch snaps.

'Well, it is,' the guy called Glenn complains.

'Yeah,' his partner sighs. 'But Mr Dowling will know if we simply go through the motions. Kinslow told us to keep searching until we're recalled. I'm not going to ignore a direct order, not from that guy.'

'Me neither,' Glenn says. 'But I think we'd be better off if the lot of us gathered round County Hall and blocked every approach. She's bound to head there, isn't she? It would make more sense than wasting our time down here.'

'Who made you the genius on the firm?' the mutant with the torch laughs. He starts down the tunnel in the direction that I've come from. 'Don't worry, I'm sure Mr Dowling or Kinslow has thought of that too. We'll be packed off there if we don't find her. But she can't have made it out of the tunnels yet, so we might as well cast around for her while she's on our turf, just in case.'

The dejected Glenn follows after his friend and my fingers clench into triumphant fists.

'I suppose,' Glenn concedes. 'But I was enjoying myself at the party. We could have sunk a few more beers before we —'

The mutant's foot catches on something and he goes down with a yelp. His partner laughs and turns to help him up. The beam of his torch swings round and I'm caught.

The taller mutant gapes at me. His jaw actually drops.

'Don't just stand there,' Glenn huffs. 'Help me . . .'

Then he notes the other guy's expression and starts to turn.

I hurl myself forward. I jump on the sprawled Glenn's back and use him as a springboard, targeting the torch. I'm a physical wreck. In a fair fight they'd take me without breaking into a sweat. But if I can

remove the light from the equation, anything could happen in the dark.

The mutant with the torch is lugging a crowbar in his other hand. He swings it at me as I jump, but he's startled, clumsy, doesn't take the fraction of a second that he needs to judge his blow and bring the bar slamming down on my head. It only grazes my shoulder while I swipe the torch away.

The torch goes flying, bounces a few times across the floor, but doesn't shatter. The beam is pointing away from us, so we're in gloom, but not total darkness.

I jab the fingers of my right hand at the mutant's head, planning to smash through his skull and destroy his brain. But in the heat of the moment I forget that some of my finger bones were mutilated by the babies. I scratch the mutant, but nothing worse than that.

He drives an elbow into my ribs. Or rather into the space where my ribs should be. Not connecting as he expected to, he's caught off balance. I grab him by the neck and force him down, using his awkward momentum against him.

Falling on top of the mutant, I extend a finger that still boasts a bone, and try to poke it through one of his eyes. Before I can, Glenn lurches at me and knocks me off his colleague.

'I've got her, Ossie!' he roars, rolling on to his back and holding me pinned on top of him. 'Finish her off!'

Ossie scrambles for his crowbar. I do my best to tear free of Glenn, but he has a firm grip on me and is shielding himself skilfully.

'Hold her still,' Ossie snarls, taking careful aim with the crowbar.

'You bloody try it if you think it's that easy,' Glenn shouts, ever the moaner.

Ossie bashes my shoulders with the crowbar a few times. I yell with pain and lash out with a kick. He dances backwards, chuckling grimly.

'Stop playing with her!' Glenn screams.

'I'm not playing,' Ossie says, cocky now that he's sized me up and seen how feeble I am. 'I just don't want to kill her if I don't have to.'

'They said that we could,' Glenn squeals. He can't see me as well as Ossie can. He doesn't know that the fight was knocked out of me long before this pair of jokers hit the scene.

'Yeah,' Ossie drawls, 'but think how pleased Mr Dowling will be if we bring her back to him in one piece.'

'We're not bloody heroes,' Glenn protests, and despite my dire situation I find myself admiring his honesty. 'Kill her while you can, you fool, before she turns the tables on us.'

'She won't be turning anything,' Ossie says, using the tip of the crowbar to poke my chin up, so that my head tilts back. His smile fades and his eyes go hard. 'But you're right. We're not heroes. Kinslow said that the vial was more important than the girl. Let's make sure she has it. If she has, I'll crack her skull open. As long as we return with the booty, we'll enjoy a hero's welcome.'

Ossie retrieves the torch while I struggle ineffectively. He shines the light on me, my hands first, then the area around me. 'Where is it?' he asks.

'Get stuffed,' I growl, lashing at Glenn's shins with my heels. He winces, but I can't do any real damage because of the strips of cloth wrapped round my feet.

'I don't want to torture you if I don't have to,' Ossie says. 'We're not like that, me and Glenn.'

'Yeah,' Glenn says earnestly. 'We'd rather kill you cleanly.'

Ossie nods. 'Tell us where the vial is and I'll make it quick. You have my word.'

'You can stick your word up your arse, along with my fist and half the arm behind it,' I jeer.

Ossie doesn't take kindly to that. His eyes narrow and he raises the bar menacingly. Then he scowls and pokes the tip into the gap where my stomach wall should be. He starts jerking it around, trying to hurt me and force me to tell them about the vial. But he's an amateur. Torture's clearly not his thing. He was telling the truth about that.

But what Ossie and Glenn lack in skill and temperament, they make up for with luck. It was the luck of the devil that they stumbled across me in the first place, and now that lucky streak strikes again as Ossie's crowbar bangs into the vial, tucked away deep inside me, and makes a dull clanging noise.

Ossie pauses. 'No way,' he mutters. Then he spies my appalled expression and hoots. 'Thanks a lot, Mrs Dowling. You've made my day.'

'What is it?' Glenn pants as Ossie bends to root through the remains of my guts. 'Is it the vial?'

'Yeah,' Ossie says. 'Has to be.'

'Well, don't go searching for it now, you dope,' Glenn yells at him. 'Finish her off first. Otherwise she'll wriggle free while you're digging around, bite through to your brain, and we'll be up the creek without a paddle.'

Ossie thinks about that and sniffs. 'You're right,' he says, standing and adjusting his grip on the crowbar. He closes one eye and lines up his shot. 'Turn your head away, Glenn. There's gonna be blood, bone and all sorts of muck flying your way in a second.'

'Just don't miss her and hit me by mistake,' Glenn says, shifting about beneath me, trying to hide his face between my shoulder blades.

'If you don't quit griping, it won't be a mistake,' Ossie says sourly, then draws back his crowbar and prepares to strike. I kick at him, hoping to catch him between the thighs, but he's alert to the threat and has positioned himself side on.

As I stare hopelessly at the raised bar, bitterly waiting for the end, cursing this sickening twist of fate, there's a flash of movement and something small hurls itself at Ossie. His face is obscured by a shimmering ball of white and red. He falls away with a yell, the crowbar and torch dropping from his fingers, hammering at whatever has attached itself to his head.

'Ossie!' Glenn screeches. 'What's going on?'

Muffled screams are Ossie's only response. He thrashes around, blood spraying from his shredded cheeks, tiny hands ripping away at his flesh, razor-sharp teeth cutting in deeper.

Glenn curses and pushes me aside. He dives for the crowbar, picks it up and strikes at the creature attacking his partner. Unfortunately for Glenn and Ossie, it smoothly pushes itself clear as the bar swings in.

43

Instead of clobbering his assailant, the bar smashes into the side of Ossie's head, and he falls to the floor, a silent heap.

'Oh no,' Glenn moans. 'Sorry, Ossie, I didn't mean to –'

Before Glenn can complete his apology, he's attacked. His face becomes the centre of a ball of moving white, glints of red among the paleness. He screams and begs for mercy, but he's wasting his breath. I've identified his foe and I know that mercy isn't in its nature.

Glenn's throat is soon ripped open and he's dead long before his attacker finishes with him and leaps aside, leaving him to collapse in a heap beside his unconscious friend.

The killer returns to Ossie and chews through his throat, then sticks a small hand up his neck and inside his head, yanking out bits of his brain, making sure he doesn't spring any surprises or send word of what happened back to base. It does the same thing with Glenn, taking no chances.

Then it turns to face me and glides closer. A tiny

figure dressed in a white gown, the material soaked with blood. Red eyes. Fangs. A hole in its thin skull, which is a smaller mirror image of the hole in my chest.

'*hello mummy*,' Holy Moly says.

And smiles.

FIVE

The baby cuddles up to me and hugs my left arm. Then it reaches up and tenderly strokes my cheek. It leaves a wet red smear behind.

'*i stopped the bad men hurting you mummy.*'

'Yes,' I sob, clutching Holy Moly tight. 'Thank you.'

'*don't be sad mummy. you're safe now. i'll look after you.*'

I'm not used to having one of the babies speak to me directly, as an individual. Normally it's always *we*, not *I*.

'Are you alone?' I ask.

'*no,*' the baby cackles. '*silly mummy. i'm with you.*'

I smile. 'I meant are any of the other babies with you?'

'*oh. no. i came by myself. we were worried about you mummy.*'

I squeeze Holy Moly tighter, then release the sweet but deadly infant and wipe some blood from its forehead and chin. 'You'll need to wash when you get back. You're dirty.'

'*it's only blood mummy,*' the baby says, then sucks a drop from its fingertip. '*yummy. but not as yummy as yummy mummy.*'

'You little charmer,' I murmur, pushing myself to my feet. I gaze at the corpses and wince. Glenn and Ossie had been all set to kill me, but they weren't the most ruthless villains I've come across. I wish we could have spared them.

'How did you find me?' I ask Holy Moly. 'Did I leave a trail?'

'*no,*' the baby says. '*we can always find mummy.*' It taps the side of its head.

The bloody telepathic link that Owl Man told me about! The babies have always been able to find me, shadowing me for much of my childhood, keeping tabs on me from a distance. Does that mean that Mr Dowling can follow me too, since we now share a link like the one I have with the babies?

'*no mummy*,' Holy Moly says, reading my troubled thoughts. '*that's not the same as our link. daddy can't search for you that way.*'

'That's a relief,' I mutter, 'though I don't suppose it makes a difference. He'll simply tag along after the others when they come looking for me.'

'*they won't do that*,' the baby says. '*i'm the only one who's coming to help mummy. only me. only holy moly.*'

It's the first time I've heard the baby use the name I gave it. I ruffle the sinister child's hair, feeling bizarrely proud, then sigh. 'The rest of them will search for me when Daddy tells them to,' I note glumly.

The baby shakes its head. '*he did ask them. he roared at us.*' Holy Moly looks rueful. '*naughty daddy. he shouted. scared his little babies. mummies and daddies should be nice all the time.*'

'Not in this world,' I say darkly, remembering my own brute of a father. 'So you're telling me you guys refused to help the clown find me?'

Holy Moly nods firmly. '*daddy wanted to kill mummy. we could see it in his head. we won't help him do that, the same way we wouldn't let you kill him. we love our yummy mummy.*'

I grin savagely, imagining how furious Mr Dowling must have been when his beloved creations rejected his orders. And he wouldn't have been able to reason with or threaten them. The babies are a law unto themselves, exactly the way he made them.

'*daddy sent his other friends after mummy instead,*' Holy Moly continues. '*we knew they'd kill mummy if they caught her. some of us said it would serve her right for hurting daddy. but we didn't mean it. we all love you mummy.*'

'Did the other babies send you to help me?' I ask.

'*no,*' Holy Moly says. '*i came because i wanted to. i often go off by myself. that's how the bad people caught me and did this.*'

The baby points to the hole in its head, reminding

50

me of the time when my friend Timothy first intro-
duced me to his incredible find. He'd discovered the
baby on a street, speared through its skull, immobile
and defenceless. We never did find out who attacked
it. I could ask now, but this isn't the time for such
enquiries.

'I need to get back to the city,' I tell Holy Moly.
'Can you help me?'

'*easy*,' the baby says confidently.

'It could be dangerous,' I warn. 'If Daddy's forces
spot us, they might punish you for helping me.'

'*they won't find us*,' Holy Moly says. '*i can see in the
dark better than they can. i can go places they don't know
about.*' The baby squeezes my hand. '*i'll look after you
mummy. i'll keep you safe. i'm a good baby i am.*'

I recall the movie, *My Fair Lady*, which my mum
loved and often made me watch with her. Thinking
about the woman in that – her catchphrase was, 'I'm
a good girl, I am' – I laugh hysterically. It's dangerous,
making this much noise, but I can't help myself.

Finally my laughter dies away and I regain control.
'OK. Where now?'

'*this way,*' Holy Moly says, starting back the way I was coming from when Ossie and Glenn found me.

'You're sure?'

'*yes. stick with holy moly. i know where i'm going.*'

I wonder for a worried moment if the baby might be planning to trick me and lead me back to Mr Dowling's base, to hand me over to its dastardly daddy. But it would have been easier to let the mutants kill me if that was the case, or just help them bind me and drag me along.

'Wait a sec.' I stop my mini guide, bending to pick up the torch. The tube inside me shifts around a bit when I do that – it must have been knocked loose in the fighting – so I take the time to nudge it firmly back into place. When my cargo is secure, I flash the torch around, to check that I'm not leaving any bloody prints, then turn it off. While it might come in handy later, for the time being we'll be safer in the darkness.

But then I see that we're not completely in the dark. Holy Moly's eyes are still glowing crimson.

'Can you make your eyes stop doing that?' I ask.

'*doing what?*' the baby replies.

'Glowing. Other people might see.'

The baby grins, showing its fangs. '*clever mummy,*' it coos, letting the red light dim and then vanish, plunging us back into fathomless black.

'Yeah, I'm a regular Einstein, me,' I croak.

'*who is einstein mummy?*' Holy Moly asks.

'I'll tell you as we walk,' I whisper, holding the baby's hand tightly so as not to get lost. 'It will help pass the time. And you can tell me about . . .' I think for a moment, then add jokingly, '. . . killing, in return.'

'*oh good,*' the baby says, taking my joke seriously, and I can sense its innocent yet chilling grin even though I can't see its face. '*i know lots about that.*'

SIX

Holy Moly is as good as its word. We slip through the tunnels like a pair of ghosts. Occasionally we hear echoes of mutants in the distance, but we don't encounter any of them as we wind our way across the city, and eventually all of the noises dwindle away completely.

Talking is an effort, so I don't tell the baby as many tales as I meant to, and I definitely don't push it to tell me any horrible stories about killing, even though it's indicated that it would be only too keen to share them with me. Holy Moly doesn't mind. It's happy to march along in silence, delighted to be of service to its *mummy*.

Sheer stubbornness keeps me going. I'm wrecked. I should lie down and rest for hours, maybe days. But I'm not convinced I'd find the strength to rise again if I stopped, so I force myself on.

I think of my reception at County Hall when I'm feeling especially weary. I try to imagine what it will be like, Dr Oystein embracing me, distraught when he sees my wounds, stunned and delighted when I reveal the vial of Schlesinger-10.

That moment will mark the beginning of our end. Once the doc has secured the vial, he'll uncork his sample of Clements-13 and the deadly fumes will start working their way through the air. He expects the virus to spread across the globe within a couple of weeks, killing every zombie that it infects. In a fortnight's time this world will belong to the living again.

I wonder if they'll mark our passing when we're gone, if there'll be plaques or statues to commemorate my name, Dr Oystein's, the rest of the Angels. Or will they try to forget about this squalid, terrible time? Maybe they'll wipe all trace of us from the history books, or claim the victory as their own. They might not want their children and grandchildren to grow up feeling indebted to a raggedy mob of the undead.

I'm not bothered either way. Like the doc, I'm not in this for the glory. I just want to do what I can to help, then check out of this hurtful world. True death will be a relief after this wretched, inbetween state.

But linking up with Dr Oystein again ... handing over the vial ... hearing the Angels cheer my name ...

Yeah, *that* will be nice. All modesty aside, I can't wait for my moment in the spotlight. I'll be getting the stamp of approval from the only people I really feel close to. The rest of the world can keep its statues and busts. If Dr Oystein says he's proud of me, and the Angels salute me, I can die a happy girl.

'*happy mummy*,' Holy Moly mumbles, reading my thoughts.

'Very happy.' I smile in the darkness. 'Are you happy too?'

'*i'm happy if mummy's happy,*' the baby says.

That simple statement makes my heart ache — or the memory of it anyway. I wish we could spare the babies. It's not fair that they have to perish along with the rest of us.

'You deserve better than this,' I tell Holy Moly. And I mean it. They might be savage little killing machines, but that's not their fault. They're capable of love too. Innocent in many ways. They could have been turned to the cause of good if they'd had Dr Oystein as a father figure instead of the psychotic clown. As things stand, they don't understand the difference between good and evil. Nobody's ever taught them.

I trudge along, my spirits sinking, thinking of all that must be sacrificed once my mission is complete. But the future of the living has to come before all other concerns. This was their planet first and we have to hand it back. That's been my priority since I returned to consciousness. Even before I stumbled upon Dr Oystein and his Angels in County Hall, I was trying to help those who had survived.

It's not that I'm a natural do-gooder. To be perfectly honest, I'm no more heroic than Ossie and Glenn were. But sometimes you get thrown in at the deep end, and you spot someone more needy and vulnerable than yourself, and you realise that if you don't put their needs first and risk your life to save theirs, then you'll eke out the rest of your days as a guilt-ridden monster. And who wants to carry on living with that sort of a millstone hanging round their neck?

As my thoughts turn more maudlin, Holy Moly helps me squeeze through a hole and we strike the tracks of a Tube line. The going is easier here. There's even the occasional light to see by. I worry that we might run into mutants – I thought Mr Dowling would have dispatched patrols in both directions along the track, figuring I'd have to connect with it at some point – but there's no sign of them.

We pass through Mansion House Station, dotted with zombies who pay us little heed. Strange to think that they'll all be stiff, harmless corpses within a few weeks, decomposing sacks of flesh and bone. Will humans come through here again one day, clean the cadavers away and restore the train service? Or will they shut these places down and leave them as mausoleums, bearers of the dark, grisly secrets of the past?

I hobble along stubbornly without pause, through the stations at Blackfriars and Temple, only stopping when I come to Embankment. This is where I'll leave the underworld behind, taking the station exit like commuters did in the old days.

'You can leave me here if you like,' I tell Holy Moly.

The baby shakes its head. *'not until we get to the city. i promised to take you to the city mummy.'*

'You'd have made a great bodyguard,' I chuckle, then lift Holy Moly up on to the platform. I didn't really need to do that – the baby can look after itself – but I wanted to feel useful.

I groan and wheeze, trying to pull myself up too. Holy Moly could help, maybe find a rope or some bags that I could use as steps, but it can see that I want to do this by myself, so it stands there quietly, leaving me to my own devices.

There are lots of zombies filling the platform, which means it must be daytime up in the world above. The living dead hordes study me with disinterest, not caring where I've come from or why I'm dressed so strangely. They have no interest in anyone that they can't eat.

Finally I clear the tracks and haul myself to my feet. I feel like I've climbed a mountain. I clasp my hands over my head and cheer jokingly at the zombies on the platform. But then I spot a figure standing close by the spot where I crawled up, and I stop in mild amazement.

It's a woman. She's dressed in white robes, and her hair is white too. I've seen her before in a station like this, when her robes and hair were a lot cleaner than they are now, but that was in Liverpool Street. She was alive when she entered the place, but she never came out. I turned her into a zombie, at her request, to prevent her brain being eaten when we were cornered by a pack of reviveds.

'*Sister Clare?*' I wheeze with disbelief.

The former leader of the Order of the Shnax

doesn't respond. She's staring off into space, like most of the zombies on the platform.

'How did you get here?' I groan, shuffling across to stand in front of her, wanting her to recognise me and respond.

The zombie says nothing. She doesn't even look at me.

I study the once barmy Sister Clare. She looks much the same as I remember. The months have been good to her. Dirtier than when she was alive, her face stained with dried blood from where she's eaten, robes filthy and ripped in several places. But otherwise there's not much difference.

'Poor cow,' I whisper, reaching up to touch her cheek. She doesn't flinch. 'You hoped you'd revitalise, but that was never an option. I didn't know it then, but I suppose it wouldn't have mattered if I had. You were trapped. There was nothing else we could have done. It was join them or become their lunch.'

Sister Clare frowns and turns her gaze on me. She's not used to talking zombies. She checks the hole where my heart should be, making sure I'm really

dead, then looks ahead again, dismissing me without thought.

I wish I could do something for her, but she seems to be in good shape. Judging by the stains around her mouth, she ate not that long ago. There isn't really any way for me to improve her sad lot.

'Come on,' I tell Holy Moly, taking its hand. 'We're on my turf now. Let me be the guide for a while.'

'*is your friend coming with us mummy?*' the baby asks.

'That crazy witch is no friend of mine,' I snort. But then I pause and glance back one last time at the statue-like Sister Clare. There's no reason why I should care about the mad zealot after she brought her grisly end down on herself, leading a group of other people to their death while she was at it. But for some strange reason I feel sorry for her.

'You'll be properly dead soon,' I murmur, insides clenching round the buried vial. 'I hope you find peace, whether it's in heaven or with your aliens. Think of me every so often if you do.'

Then, having wasted enough time on the undead woman, I work my way up through the station, squeezing by the zombies who pack the platform and tunnels. They're even crowding the escalators, sitting or standing on the steps, gazing blankly off into the distance like Sister Clare was. I wish the escalators were working – what I wouldn't give for a smooth ride up out of the depths – but they're as lifeless as the people stacked along them.

I limp onwards and upwards. Holy Moly ducks in and out between my legs as I walk, treating this as a game. I'm not looking any further ahead than the next step, not wanting to focus on how far I have to go, knowing I'd lose heart if I stopped to check. What I can't see can't freak me out.

Eventually I make it to the top, and I'm more relieved than I should be. I was beginning to think that I'd truly died, that this was hell, an endless series of steps that I'd have to spend all of eternity climbing.

'That was easy, wasn't it?' I mutter.

'*yes,*' Holy Moly says, missing the sarcasm.

The ticket barriers are open, so at least I don't have that hassle to deal with. We push through and out of the riverbank exit, into sunlight. The light hurts my eyes, but not as much as I thought it would, and it starts to get dimmer after a few seconds, cancelling out the headache that I normally get when travelling by day.

The dimness confuses me until I recall the special contact lenses that Mr Dowling stuck in when he rebuilt my ruined body. They must feature an automatic tinting system. I'm still not comfortable in the sunlight, but I can deal with it and see much more clearly than I could before.

'Thanks, hubby,' I whisper, and spread my arms wide, feeling like Lazarus reborn. I'm sure I'm wearing a goofy smile but I don't care. This is glorious after the darkness of that underworld realm. Even the itching isn't as bad as it used to be, probably because of all the replacement flesh that the clown grafted on to me.

'*shall i leave you here mummy?*' Holy Moly asks.

That surprises me. The baby seems almost eager to

66

be rid of me. But then I recall that I asked it to lead me safely to the city. Now that we're here, it clearly thinks that its job is done. It's not looking to abandon me — it just assumes that I have no more need of it and want to be by myself. The babies are nothing if not literal.

'Stick with me a few more minutes,' I tell it, heading under a bridge to the right of the station. 'I want to show you where I live. It's a lovely sight. Let me share it with you. Your reward for helping me out.'

'*silly mummy*,' Holy Moly beams. '*i don't need a reward. i love you mummy.*' But the baby comes with me anyway, to humour me. I've a feeling it would go anywhere I asked it to go.

A railway line crosses the river here. There are footbridges attached to both sides. I limp across to the one that faces Westminster. Steps lead up to the bridge, but there's also a lift. I say a little prayer that it's working and, what do you know, the gods are smiling on me for once.

'Going up,' I laugh as we ascend.

Holy Moly looks the teeniest bit scared. I don't

think the baby has been in a lift before. I tickle the little one's belly to distract it and it laughs with utter delight.

The lift stops and we shuffle out. I pick up Holy Moly and stagger to the rails, to point towards the Houses of Parliament, then across the river to the gleaming London Eye, County Hall lying just behind it.

'There,' I tell Holy Moly. 'That's where Mummy and her friends live. Isn't it the most wonderful place you've ever . . .'

My words tail off. It's a sunny day in London. The rays pick out the Eye and the building to its rear. The pair of landmarks shine majestically, as if the daylight was created to highlight their glory.

But, with the help of my contact lenses, I can see other things just as clearly — mutants, zombies and scores of babies, each of the infants an exact replica of Holy Moly, only without a hole in its head.

Mr Dowling's troops, gathered in their grisly might, have formed a ring around County Hall and are in the process of overrunning the complex. As I watch with stunned horror, they dash in and out of the entrances, smashing windows, killing anyone they find.

The clown and his lethal posse have launched an attack on County Hall, the home of Dr Oystein and his Angels. And, by the look of things, the battle has already been decided. The good guys have lost. The bad guys have won.

I think of the vial inside my stomach. I stare at the sickening scenes across the river. I lower my head and make a weak keening noise, not cursing this twist of fate, not mourning those I've probably lost, just thinking numbly — who the hell can I turn to now?

SEVEN

Several corpses have been heaped in the middle of Jubilee Gardens, a small park between the bridge and County Hall. Furniture has been stacked nearby, and many mutants are adding to the pile, racing in and out of the building with tables, chairs and bedding, which they deposit on the growing mound.

As other mutants soak the pyre with petrol, one lights a torch, then steps forward and shouts a warning. The rest of them scatter and the torch is hurled on to the primed furniture. A bonfire explodes into life. The mutants cheer and applaud.

Then they start tossing the bodies of my slain comrades on to the flames.

'*toasty,*' Holy Moly murmurs approvingly, but I don't react, reminding myself that the baby's been brought up to see nothing amiss in atrocities like this.

Despite my improved vision, I can't see from here if the Angels being fed to the fire were some of my room-mates, Shane, Ashtat, Carl, or others I felt close to. And I don't want to know. Better the corpses remain faceless. That way I don't have to mourn them.

I spot an Angel climbing on to the roof in an attempt to get away. It looks like a girl but I can't be sure. She stumbles off in the direction of St Thomas's Hospital but doesn't get far. Babies follow and launch themselves in a deadly swarm at the helpless revitalised, dragging her down and ripping into her.

I spy another Angel, a boy, in a pod on the London Eye. He must have been on watch when the attack commenced, so it can't have been more than half an hour ago, which is roughly the time it takes for a pod to complete a revolution.

The Angel is gazing down on a group of mutants. They're packing all sorts of weapons and howling gleefully, waving at the trapped boy, making crude gestures. Some begin to climb up to the pod, impatient, eager to strike the first blow.

As mutants scrabble across the top of the pod and try to smash through the glass, the Angel makes a crude gesture of his own, then drives the bones sticking out of his fingers through his skull. The mutants screech spitefully, but he ignores them and digs around inside his head. Moments later he drops to the floor of the pod, set free from the torment which would otherwise have awaited him.

I hate being a helpless observer. I want to dash across the bridge, cut through Jubilee Gardens, fight and die with those who have become my family over the last few months.

But I don't have the energy for a stylish finale. If I start limping across this walkway, I'll be spotted long before I reach the other side. Mutants will flood the bridge and either kill me or haul me back for Mr Dowling to deal with.

So I hold my ground and watch numbly as County Hall falls to its foes. I'm surprised they were able to take it so easily. I thought the Angels would have offered more resistance. Master Zhang trained us to be clinical fighting machines. We should have been able to at least trouble the mutants and babies. But it looks like they took this place as swiftly and casually as they took Battersea Power Station.

I wonder if Dr Oystein has been killed. There aren't that many dead Angels outside the building, so most must be lining the corridors inside. Dr Oystein's corpse almost surely lies among one of the groups, unless he happened to be at his secret lab when Mr Dowling surged up out of the depths.

If the doc was here when the invasion began, how did he react? Seeing that the end was upon him, did he uncork his vial of Clements-13, figuring Mr Dowling wouldn't have attacked unless he'd been robbed of his sample of Schlesinger-10? Maybe ultimate victory is already ours, despite the casualties and the loss of our base. Perhaps this is merely Mr Dowling's compensation prize, annihilation of his most hated enemy before he falls foul of the unleashed virus and drops dead in a matter of days.

Then again, Dr Oystein never told us where his vial of Clements-13 was stored. I'm sure he has some in his hidden laboratory, but did he keep another vial on him, or tucked away in a safe nook in County Hall? I'm guessing he did, in order to be ready for a surprise attack like this, but I can't be certain.

Mr Dowling can't have been certain either. That's why he never struck the first blow. But now, robbed of his ultimate deterrent, he's had to gamble. I left him with no other choice.

Understanding the clown as intimately as I do, I knew that his first task would be to find me and retrieve his vial of Schlesinger-10, to re-establish the status quo. He likes things the way they've been since the world fell, the war between the living and the undead, the chaos and disorder.

But I didn't consider what he'd do when his mutants failed to track me down. He must have decided to strike immediately before I returned to County Hall. He probably figured that he was definitely dead if he waited. At least this way he had a chance.

I should have anticipated this. If I'd been thinking clearly, I would have acted more swiftly, made for the surface as soon as I could, maybe sent Holy Moly on ahead of me to warn Dr Oystein and tell him to clear out. I thought I had time to play with. I was wrong.

'It's a bloody mess,' I sob, turning away from the carnage, sick of it all, not wanting to torture myself any further.

'*mummy?*' Holy Moly asks, surprised by my sadness. The baby doesn't understand why I'm miserable. The slaughter across the river is nothing more than a jolly piece of theatre as far as it's concerned, par for the course when their father is abroad. '*what's wrong mummy? don't cry. we don't like it when you cry. we love you mummy.*'

'I'm OK,' I lie. 'Just sad because my friends are dead.'

'*everything dies mummy,*' Holy Moly says.

'Is that supposed to comfort me?' I snap.

Holy Moly nods sweetly. '*yes.*'

I suppress a grimace. 'I know you mean well, but I'd rather be by myself right now. Will you leave me, like you were going to a while ago?'

'*if that's what you want . . .*' Holy Moly says uncertainly, worried about me now.

'It is,' I say firmly. 'You guided me to safety. You're a good boy . . . or girl . . . or whatever the hell you are. I'll be fine on my own.'

'*ok mummy,*' Holy Moly says and sets off across the bridge, moving with its characteristic eerie smoothness and speed.

'Wait!' I call the baby back. 'Where are you going?'

'*there,*' Holy Moly says, pointing at County Hall. '*i want to be with the others. they look like they're having fun.*'

'I'm sure they are,' I say bitterly, finding it hard not to hate the baby right now. 'But will you do me a favour?'

'*of course,*' it squeals, excited to be of service.

'Will you go the other way?' I ask. 'Back underground, to wait for the rest of them in Daddy's den?'

Holy Moly stares at me, its pale forehead wrinkling. '*but i'll miss the fighting mummy.*'

'That's not a bad thing,' I tell it. 'I don't want you to fight.'

'*why not?*'

I pause, wondering how to explain the difference between good and evil. In the end I decide it's a hopeless task, that I'd only confuse the poor thing if I began lecturing it.

'I'm worried you might get hurt,' I say instead.

The baby giggles. '*silly mummy.*'

'Silly as they come.' I smile stiffly. 'But please, do this for me. I'll be happy if I know you're safe.'

'*ok mummy,*' Holy Moly sighs, and sets off in the other direction, back the way we came. The baby stops at the lift door and stares solemnly at the button. Turns and looks at me. '*can i use the stairs instead of the small room? i didn't like the small room mummy.*'

I nod. 'The stairs will be fine.'

'*thank you mummy,*' Holy Moly says, trotting to the top step.

'Wait.' I stop the baby again. It looks back questioningly. I'm tired and I don't want to think about the future, but I must. I know that Dr Oystein would want me to fight on, even when all else seems lost. There's not much I can do by myself to thwart the forces of wickedness and madness, but maybe I can throw a spanner in the works, or at least cause them a few sleepless nights.

'Come here,' I call to Holy Moly, crouching down and leaning back against the bars which support the railing that runs across the bridge. 'I want to make my last will and testament, and I'd like you to be my executor.'

'*i don't understand mummy*,' Holy Moly says.

'I know,' I laugh softly. 'But it won't take me long to explain . . .'

EIGHT

I rest on the bridge after Holy Moly has slipped away, listening to the roars, screams and crackle of flames in the near distance. The mutants have started fires inside County Hall, hell-bent on burning the place to the ground. I don't think they stand a hope of doing that, but they can certainly gut a lot of it if they carry on as they've begun.

As I'm gathering myself for my final push, I think about Dr Oystein and the Angels, Ciara and Reilly, Master Zhang. Are any of them alive? Did some of them make it out before the net closed? If so, how many will survive the next few challenging weeks, robbed of their base and support?

I could easily stay where I am and brood, but since I don't want to be discovered by a stray mutant or baby, I crawl to the lift (in my state, the stairs would be too much of a challenge) and return to ground level.

I limp along beside the river, heading east simply because that's the most direct route out of here. I stick close to the buildings on my left, hugging the shadows, making sure no one on the South Bank can spot me.

I want to feel worse than I do, have a nervous breakdown, beat the pavement with my fists, howl at the sky and demand justice from God. But I've endured so many terrible things in recent times that I can't work up to a hysterical high. I've lost my family and everyone I cared about, been tortured by one homicidal maniac, and married to another. Ever since I was turned into a zombie, it seems that all the world has wanted to do is pummel me, cast me aside and leave me to wander on my own through the urban wilderness.

In the past I had hope to keep me going. The hope that I might be able to help the living, that there was a place for me in this savage new society, that I could be of worth.

That hope has been cut away from me. This was one blow too many. It's not the physical pain that has left me feeling hollow inside, or the loss of my friends, or the fact that I'm all on my own.

No, the reason I feel like I'm all washed up is that this has happened to me over and over again. The forces of destiny or luck are not on my side. Everything in nature seems to be lined up against me.

Why push on and fight for a world that clearly doesn't want me, that has punished me at every well-meaning turn? I'm not dumb. I get the message. I tried to play the part of a hero, even though it wasn't in my genes, but some higher power has decided I'm not fit for that role. It wants the glory to go to someone else. I understand. In truth, that's the way it should be. A hero should be someone proud and noble, not a loud-mouthed girl who was too afraid to stand up to a racist, who threw an innocent boy to a pack of zombies because she didn't have the guts to disobey her bullying father.

Heh. It always comes back to Tyler Bayor. I suppose it always should. That's when I cast my humanity aside. Everything since then has been an attempt to make up for that foul deed, to redeem myself. But some creeps aren't worthy of redemption. Time for me to find a hole where I can curl up and die.

Except I won't truly die, will I? I can lie there, starve and wait for my senses to crumble, but that's not the same thing. I'll carry on as a mindless zombie in that case and maybe kill again one day.

I want out. I *need* to get out. If I could rely on the mutants and babies to kill me, I'd throw myself into the battle at County Hall and perish with my friends and allies, but there's a good chance that they'd take me captive and deliver me to their master instead, and who knows where things would go from there. No, if I want this job done properly, I have to do it myself. I'll find a drill or a chainsaw and bore into my skull. Hell, even a good, sharp knife will suffice.

Having made up my mind, all that remains is to choose my spot. Most people aren't that fortunate when it's their time to pass on from this realm. They simply drop wherever fate decrees. But, whether I deserve it or not, I have a choice. I can do it somewhere random or I can pick a place that means something to me.

I think about it as I shuffle along. Both options have their appeal. A random location would allow me to do it sooner rather than later, and I think it would be fitting if I died in a lonely, unmarked place. After all, isn't that where all failures should wind up?

But at the same time, if there *is* a higher power, one that's been stacking the deck of cards against me, I wouldn't mind sticking a couple of fingers up at it before I check out. B Smith — rebel to the end!

I decide on my old flat in the East End. I've had several bases since then, but that's the spot I always think of as home. I didn't realise it at the time, but that's where I was at my happiest. I had plenty of lousy experiences there too, when Dad terrorised Mum and me, but that's where I was loved (and bullied), where I was safe (most of the time), where I was free to grow and learn and live (under the thumb of an outright racist).

Yeah, the flat will be a good finishing point. A neat way to draw a line under my existence. Pick up a sharp tool along the way. Drag myself up the stairs. Crawl into my old room. Lie on my bed, stare at the ceiling, go to work on my head, churn up my brain and let it all end. Rot away slowly until I'm only dust, a dwindling memory in the dusty database of the universe.

Perversely, I cheer up once I've made my decision. I even hum as I plod along. '*Heigh-ho, heigh-ho, it's off to die I go.*'

I have a goal now, and it's not the sort of epic goal that I've been chasing since I linked up with Dr

Oystein. No more saving the world for this undead girl. All I have to worry about is making it home and signing off. That's the sort of challenge I was born to deal with.

Watch out, afterlife — here I come!

NINE

The walk east is taking an age. It's a good job I'm not in a hurry. I doubt any tourist ever went along this slowly in the past, and that's bearing in mind that sightseers in London weren't known for their speed — they used to drive us locals mad if we got stuck behind a pack of them on a busy street.

I'm enjoying the river views. I find the Thames oddly peaceful and calming. I don't normally pay much attention to it, but it demands my focus today on the long, laborious march home. Maybe it's because the serene, constantly flowing water reminds me of the journey my soul is soon to embark on, and I want to believe that my spirit will drift along effortlessly like this when it's set free from my shambolic form. A fool's dream, probably, but a nice image to dwell on while I'm crawling ever eastwards in a fog of nightmarish pain.

I stop when I reach the Millennium Bridge, and on an impulse decide to cross the river to the South Bank. I've come a long way from Westminster, so I no longer have to worry about running into mutants, and it's a more interesting walk on the south side.

I drag myself across the bridge and step off in the shadow of the towering Tate Modern. If I was in better shape, I might pop in to check out the exhibits, but this most certainly isn't a day to be visiting art galleries.

I trudge past the Globe, where I spot a zombie in Shakespearean garb, probably an actor from back in the day, standing just inside the entrance. He's making odd, jerky movements with his head and arms, and I realise after a few confused moments that he's trying to act out a scene from a dimly remembered play. As drained as I am, I stop and clap slowly. The actor's face lights up with the memory of applause-filled times, and he awkwardly bows towards me. That's my good deed for the day taken care of.

I detour down a dark, cobbled street, past an old prison complex that would have been a perfect jail for the likes of Dan-Dan and my other foes. I lose sight of the river for a while, before linking up with the path again just past London Bridge.

As I make my slow, shuffling way along the river-bank, I think about where I can pick up a decent power tool. I'd like to clock out in style. A really good, strong drill that will arrow clean through my skull, leaving only the smallest, most discreet of holes behind when I yank it out and drop it while I thrash around and die.

I know this area well, both from my human years and the time I spent exploring here over the past months. I'm trying to remember where the best DIY shops are located, but I'm drawing a blank, finding it hard to focus in my sorry, stressed state.

'What a time to develop Alzheimer's,' I growl, jabbing at my head with a fist, trying to knock my senses back into place. My fingers brush against the nails which Dan-Dan hammered into my scalp. I pause, wondering if I can drive the nails in deeper, maybe by banging the top of my head against a wall.

'It could work,' I mutter. 'Puncture the brain, drop me in my tracks, no need to worry about my hand shaking and misdirecting a drill. But what if it doesn't quite kill me? I might just scramble my senses, become a wandering moron.'

As I'm picking at the nails and mumbling to myself like a madwoman, I catch sight of a familiar vessel and draw bitterly to a halt. HMS *Belfast*, where I first met Dan-Dan and the other accursed members of the Board. The cruiser was a popular tourist draw in the old days, but for me it's a place of painful memories.

I glare at the deserted ship as if it was responsible for the foul crew it played host to, recalling the duels, the zombies I was forced to kill, the torment the humans put me through. I didn't know it at the time, but worse was to come. That being said, this was where my problems with the Board began, so I hate this place even more than Battersea Power Station.

The memories make me wonder about Justin Bazini and Vicky Wedge, last seen fleeing from Mr Dowling's army in Battersea, presumed dead but unconfirmed. And Barnes, the American soldier of fortune who took me captive, but later turned hero. When he bid me farewell, he was setting off to try and save his son. I hope he made it, that they were reunited and are lounging on the beach of an island free from zombies. But this world being what it is, I suspect that isn't the case, that Barnes came a cropper, while Bazini and Wedge are living the high life in Buckingham Palace or some other suitably stylish spot.

As I'm considering the fates of my old enemies, I spot movement on the deck of the *Belfast*. A couple of people are playing with a ball, throwing it to one another.

I'm instantly wary. Backing up from the edge of the path, I resume my shuffle east. I'm bent over almost double with pain, which is good. That makes me less of a conspicuous target. I don't want to be spotted by whoever is on board what should be a ghost ship.

But to my utter lack of surprise, Dame Fortune deserts me yet again. As I'm glancing backwards, one of the people on the deck misses the ball. It bounces over their head and they turn to chase it. Even though I'm almost clear of the cruiser, he or she spies me on the path and stops to check me out.

I carry on towards Tower Bridge, draping my left arm over my head — it looks as if I'm doing it to protect my face from the sun, but it also allows me to twist my head around and slyly keep an eye on the *Belfast*. I'm hoping the pair with the ball have mistaken me for an ordinary zombie. There's no reason why they shouldn't. In my rough state I look even worse than most reviveds. I'd be hard to peg as a revitalised up close, never mind from a distance.

The person who failed to catch the ball shields their eyes and stares. I know the watcher can't see me in detail, given how far away I am and the fact that my back is to them. I don't have anything to worry about.

But then the bugger raises a pair of binoculars and I groan. I can predict what's coming next and, sure enough, a moment later the person shouts and gestures. He or she is joined by their companion, and that one has binoculars too. They study me for a few seconds, then cast the binoculars aside and race across the deck, no doubt heading for the gangplank.

I think about making a dash for it. There are lots of small streets and buildings on the far side of Tower Bridge where I could hide. But I don't have the energy for a chase. Better to make a stand and face whatever manner of foe the universe has chosen to pit against me this time.

I limp along a bit further and draw to a halt outside the weirdly shaped glass structure of City Hall, the mayor's old stomping ground. This seems as fitting a spot to fight as any. A good place to fall if it's my time.

I turn stiffly and watch the pair from the *Belfast* hurrying towards me. I try to crack my knuckles, but they only make a soft, soggy sound when I stretch them. I laugh softly and let my hands fall by my sides. I let my head hang too, not concerned about the identity of my assailants, figuring they can announce themselves if they want to. I won't do them the courtesy of being curious.

They come to a stop a few metres from me. I can't see their faces but I can feel them gawping. I grin tightly, saying nothing, waiting for them to make their move.

Finally one of them says, '*B?*'

It's a girl's voice, not what I was expecting.

I don't answer. I think I recognise the voice, but I don't want to raise my hopes, sure they'll be dashed if I do.

'Is that you, B?' the other one asks, and this time it's a boy. I'm sure I recognise his voice too, but again I'm worried that I might be imagining things. Maybe my metallic ears are distorting the sounds, making me hear what I want to hear.

'Who wants to know?' I grunt.

'It's us,' the girl says.

'The twins,' the boy adds.

At that, I can't help myself. I look up, expecting my eyes to contradict what I've heard. But, to my surprise, the vision matches the voices. A boy and girl a few years younger than me, with blond hair and fair skin. They helped clean me up when I first crawled out of a Groove Tube all those months ago.

'Cian?' I say dumbly. 'Awnya? What are you guys doing here?'

'Waiting for you,' Awnya says.

'And playing catch,' Cian chuckles.

The twins sweep forward and hug me. I can only stare at the top of their heads like a dope, wondering if I'm dreaming.

Then Cian says, 'What happened to your stomach?'

And Awnya says, 'Ew! Gross!'

And suddenly I know it's real. With a cry of shock

and delight, I wrap my arms round them, and for the longest time I just stand there, hugging the young twins hard, without a single other care in the world, all thoughts of suicide forgotten, lost for a short, blissful period to an emotion I thought I'd never feel again in this undead life.

Happiness.

TEN

Eventually the twins tire of the hugging and let go. I would have been content to hug them forever, but I don't want to appear like some kind of desperate creep, so I grin shakily and force a weak chuckle.

'You guys will never know how relieved I am to see you,' I mutter.

'Who did you think we were?' Cian asks.

'Bad people?' Awnya laughs.

'The very worst,' I tell them, my smile slipping.

The twins see the pain on my face. They study my

wounds, this time seriously, saying nothing, concern and compassion in their gaze.

'Are you OK, B?' Awnya asks.

'Of course she's not OK,' Cian huffs. 'Look at the hole in her stomach. How could anyone be *OK* when they look like that?'

Awnya ignores her brother. 'How bad is it?'

'Pretty damn bad,' I admit with a grimace. 'But I've plugged up the worst of the damage and made it this far. I can battle on a bit further.'

'Maybe we could find something to patch you up more efficiently,' Awnya says. 'There are some pharmacies close by. We could get proper bandages, plasters, anything you need.'

'It'll take more than that to put me together again,' I sniff.

'I think even all the king's horses and all the king's men would have a tough time with this one,' Cian nods.

'Idiot,' Awnya snorts, and we exchange a look that girls everywhere have been sharing since the dawn of time — *boys*!

'So, all kidding aside, what were you doing on the *Belfast*?' I ask.

'Waiting for you,' Cian says.

'Really,' Awnya adds.

I frown. 'How did you know I'd come this way?'

'We didn't,' Awnya says.

'But Dr Oystein hoped you'd return to a place you were familiar with,' Cian explains.

'He posted Angels here, Battersea Power Station, your old flat,' Awnya says. 'Anywhere he thought you might turn up if you managed to escape.'

'He didn't think I was a lost cause?' I ask hoarsely.

'He feared the worst,' Awnya sighs.

'But he said if anyone could get out of that mad clown's den, it was you,' Cian smirks.

'He never gave up on you,' Awnya says softly.

'He prayed and had faith,' Cian whispers.

'And his prayers have been answered,' Awnya finishes with a shy smile.

I shake my head wordlessly. I'm overwhelmed. I knew the doc loved us, but for him to pin this much hope on me, to keep the faith even though he must have known the odds were stacked sky-high against me . . .

When I was a child, I believed completely in my dad. I thought he'd always be there for me, that no matter what happened he would turn up to save me if I got into trouble. It's been a long time since I had that sort of unreserved belief in a person, but Dr Oystein has restored it, made me feel like a kid again, in all the best ways.

'That crazy, beautiful old saint,' I croak. Then I remember what I witnessed at County Hall and my happiness evaporates. 'But he should have been looking out for himself. County Hall has fallen. Mr Dowling attacked. I saw his troops killing everyone. Dr Oystein is probably dead. He should have focused on his defences, not wasted his time on a stray wretch like me.'

'Easy, B,' Awnya says. 'The doc is fine.'

'He doesn't overlook anything,' Cian says proudly.

I stare at them uncertainly. 'But County Hall *did* fall. I saw it, just before I came here. The mutants overran it. There were dead bodies piled outside. Mr

Dowling's crew were throwing them on to a bonfire.'

Cian and Awnya both look downcast.

'Dr Oystein thought that might happen,' Cian says.

'He wanted to withdraw everyone,' Awnya says.

'But Master Zhang convinced him to leave a small group of Angels behind,' Cian goes on. 'To make it look like we were still based in the building.'

'He didn't want our enemies to know that we'd moved,' Awnya says.

'The doc wasn't keen,' Cian says glumly.

'But in the end he agreed to Master Zhang's plan,' Awnya concludes.

'What plan?' I snap. 'What are you talking about? This isn't making sense.'

Awnya casts a disapproving look in my direction. 'You should know that Dr Oystein thinks of everything.'

Cian nods. 'He figured we were in trouble as soon as he heard that Mr Dowling had kidnapped you, and he immediately made plans to move us out of County Hall.'

I stare at the twins. 'You're telling me the doc upped sticks?'

'Yes,' Awnya says.

'Why?' I croak. 'How did he know that Mr Dowling would attack?'

'I'm not sure,' Awnya says. 'Maybe he just had a feeling.'

'Or maybe he has spies among the clown's people,' Cian grunts.

'Either way, he slipped us out of there,' Awnya says. 'We relocated to a base he'd set up ages ago in case we ever needed to evacuate in a hurry.'

'County Hall might have fallen but the doc hasn't,' Cian smirks.

'He's safe,' Awnya agrees. 'And he's waiting for us to bring you to him.'

My mind is reeling. I don't know how the doc saw this one coming! Then again, I shouldn't be too surprised that he was several steps ahead of me. He's not a dumb foot soldier. It's his job to think things through and make plans in advance, taking all the variables into consideration. Maybe he knew that Mr Dowling wanted to marry me. Maybe he gambled that I'd accept the clown's proposal for one reason or another, and figured there was a chance that I'd find out where his vial of Schlesinger-10 was stored and manage to steal off with it. Relocating his base on a hunch was a brave, bold move, but it wouldn't be the first time that Dr Oystein pinned everything on a gut instinct.

I'm so happy that I want to hop around like a lunatic and shout for joy until I'm hoarse. But I can't summon the strength. The best I can manage is a wry smile and a very weak-sounding, 'Wow.'

'Come on,' Awnya says. 'We'll take you with us. Dr Oystein will be sad when he finds out those we left behind were killed, but he'll be delighted to see you again.'

'This is incredible,' I chuckle. 'I can't wait to see him, but how far is it to these new quarters of yours?'

'Not far,' Awnya says. 'It's in Bow, in an old factory where they used to make matches.'

That rings a bell. 'I think I know the place you're talking about. It was turned into flats. The Bow Quarter, near Victoria Park?'

'Yes,' Cian says, impressed. 'How did you know?'

'I used to live over that way. I've passed it loads of times. It was an eye-catching place.'

I consider the walk to Bow. The twins are right, it's not far away, an easy hour and a bit if I was in good shape. But in my current condition it's an unappealing prospect.

'I'm not up for the journey,' I tell them. 'It would take hours. I can barely manage a crawl.'

'We could carry you,' Awnya suggests.

'I don't think so.'

'We're strong enough,' Cian growls, puffing himself up.

'I'm sure you are,' I reply, 'but I'd slow you down, and speed is important. Mr Dowling's mutants will start looking for me again when they're finished at County Hall. The sooner I can link up with Dr Oystein, the better.'

Cian rubs his chin thoughtfully. 'So what do you want us to do? We can't just leave you here, injured and alone.'

'Tell you what,' I decide, thinking about the route

east. 'You guys can help me get to Brick Lane. You need to pass close by it anyway. There's an old brewery there that I know well, where I can lay low. Drop me off and I'll wait there for you to bring Dr Oystein to me.'

'Are you sure?' Awnya frowns. 'Maybe it would be safer if one of us stayed with you.'

'No,' I tell her. 'You two work better as a team. I'll be fine by myself. It's a nice place to rest. Mr Dowling has no reason to suspect I'll head there.'

The twins glance at one another, think about it, then nod.

'OK,' Awnya says.

'If that's what you want,' Cian chirps.

Then they move to either side of me, link arms with mine and we're off, like Dorothy and her friends on the road to Oz. But there's no way I'm going to sing 'Follow the Yellow Brick Road'. I was always a lousy singer, even when I had lungs to sing with.

ELEVEN

It takes even longer than I anticipated to cross the river and complete the short march to Brick Lane. The twins are shocked when they see how hard I find it to drag one leg after the other. Awnya suggests I stop before Brick Lane and rest up in the Tower of London or Aldgate. But I have the Truman Brewery in my head now, and the lure of it keeps me going. I want to lie back somewhere familiar, study Timothy's paintings, reflect on all that has happened. I'll feel safe there. I'd be uneasy anywhere else.

The twins are wearing hats, sunglasses and jackets to protect them from the daylight. They offer to find the same for me, but I barely notice the discomfort that walking around in the sunshine usually causes. I have far more painful crosses to bear.

Eventually we get to the turning for Brick Lane and I smile painfully. 'Home sweet home. You can leave me here. No need to come all the way.'

'Are you sure?' Awnya asks.

'What if you're attacked?' Cian says.

'And what if a meteor falls on me?' I respond tetchily. 'Look, even if I collapse, I won't fall far short, so you'll know where to find me. By the time I get there, you'll be halfway to Bow. Coming any further with me would be a waste of time.'

'In that case we shouldn't have bothered bringing you this far,' Cian says and I feel like giving him a slap. But then he sticks out his tongue and laughs, and I forgive him.

'Take care, B,' Cian says.

'I will.'

'You're sure you don't want one of us to stay with you?' Awnya asks.

'I'm sure.'

The twins shrug and turn to leave.

'Hey.' I stop them. 'Thanks. You saved me. I won't forget it.'

'You'd have been fine,' Cian snorts.

I shake my head slowly. He catches my dark look and his grin fades.

'You guys hurry on back,' I mutter.

They wave at me and set off, fast as hares now that they don't have me to slow them down. I watch them depart, feeling lonely again, but nowhere near as lost as I did before they linked up with me and told me hope was still alive. Then I turn into Brick Lane and start hobbling.

I pass the first of the legions of curry houses which this street was once famous for, and remember a conversation with Timothy, when he offered to cook me a meal. The artist was as loony as Mr Dowling in his own way, but sweet with it. I still miss him, even though I didn't get to know him that well.

I spot a few zombies lurking in the shadows of the restaurants. They can tell with a glance that I'm one of them, so they pay me no mind.

It's only as I draw close to my goal that I recall the last time I was here, the day that Mr Burke tried to kill Dr Oystein. My old teacher had found me in the Brewery, acting as a makeshift curator, taking care of Timothy's paintings. Rage was with him, helping cart a trolley full of folders across the city from wherever they'd dug them up. Rage and I left Burke there, poring over the paperwork.

The next time I saw him, he was insane. He tried to shoot the doc. While subduing Burke, I accidentally infected him and he turned into a zombie. We knew that Mr Dowling must have got hold of him and fried his brain, because the very last thing he wheezed to me before he lost his humanity was the clown's name.

Dr Oystein was keeping the undead Billy Burke in County Hall at my request, on the off chance that he might revitalise. I wonder if he brought the zombie teacher with him when they moved base, or if he left Burke behind, or set him free. I must ask him when we've finished discussing our other business. I liked Burke and feel guilty for robbing him of his life. I want to do right by him.

The front door of the building is open. There are several zombies on the ground floor, standing or sitting, staring off blankly into space, waiting for night to fall. I could shoo them out, but they're not bothering me, so I leave them be.

I shuffle forward, meaning to crawl up the stairs to check that Timothy's paintings are in good condition. The artist loved his drawings. They gave his life meaning. I hope Mr Dowling's mutants didn't destroy or disfigure any of them when they found Burke here and went to work on him.

Then I spot a few folders lying open on the floor and pause. They're some of the files from the trolley that Burke and Rage were lugging through the streets on that awful day. I don't know what my ex-teacher was hoping to find in them, and I don't really care, but the sight of the folders distresses me.

They remind me of my history with Mr Burke, his grisly conversion, the role I played in it. I decide to tidy the place up, return the folders to the trolley, maybe push it out of here if I have the strength. At least that way I won't have to be forcibly reminded of the good friend that I lost.

With a groan, I bend and pick up the nearest folder. I stare at it sadly. Perhaps these were the pages Burke was looking at when Mr Dowling snuck up on him and struck. The final words he read as a living human, unaware that the end was so close.

Curious, I flick through the pages, trying to put myself in Burke's shoes, to imagine what he might have been thinking about. The pages are densely packed with small print, lots of paragraphs crammed in, technical jargon. I can't understand most of it and I start to lay the folder aside.

Then I spot a name that stops me — *Dowling*.

I raise the folder again and try reading the paragraph from the first line, but it doesn't make sense taken out of context, so I flick back to the beginning of the chapter and start from there.

I'm not a quick reader. Normally it takes me a long time to plough through a chunk of text. But, as the significance of what I'm reading sinks in, I find myself flying through the pages.

After a while, I put the folder down and numbly pick up one of the others. Again I find the name of Dowling. It appears often on the pages. If I'd been putting these dossiers together, I'd have been more cautious. I wouldn't have plastered names across them. But the people compiling these reports were confident that they would never be read by the general public. They knew that if all went according to plan, there soon wouldn't even *be* a general public.

Because these are the blueprints for the end of mankind, records of the build-up to the release of the zombie virus. They chart all sorts of activities that were going on worldwide in the months and years before that apocalyptic day. I knew that the virus had been spread on purpose, that corrupt, powerful people had used it to cement their stranglehold on the world. But I had no idea it was this convoluted or that the players involved were so numerous or devious.

In a hollow daze I pick up another folder to find more of the same. Details of the main participants, politicians, soldiers, scientists, engineers, media moguls. Drawings of complexes like the one I was housed in as a zom head, along with plans for the development of zombie-free islands. Lists of the building materials that they sourced, supplies of food, drink and ammunition that they stockpiled.

The files show how the virus was replicated, samples being delivered to major cities and towns, how the global release was coordinated, in many cases using stooges who had no idea what they were unleashing. The pages explain how lines of communication were brought crashing down, to make it harder for the survivors to get in contact with one another and organise a fightback.

There are figures outlining payments made. Those who were corrupt were bribed. Those who wouldn't play ball were discredited, humiliated, financially crippled. In certain cases assassins were hired to execute those with a conscience who were considered a problem.

I don't know where Burke found these folders, but they're dynamite. Maybe they were stored in a military safe house that had fallen to Mr Dowling's mutants or a surprise zombie attack. He might have learnt of the whereabouts of such places when he was working with the army as a spy for Dr Oystein. I bet Burke didn't realise what he'd laid his hands on until he started reading. His mind must have boggled.

What did he feel when he saw the names and started piecing it all together? Terror? Disgust? Panic? I'm not sure, but I know by what happened in County Hall what he felt in the end — hatred, fury and madness.

I haven't got to that stage yet. I'm still in shock, unable to believe what I'm reading, even though it's all laid out clearly. I want to be wrong. I want this to be a smokescreen, something cooked up by vile, merciless individuals, a web of discrediting lies to entrap those who would oppose them.

But I'm not *that* dumb. I can recognise the truth

when it's put before me. Even though I wish to all the gods that I couldn't.

Names. It all comes back to names. Thousands of people are listed in the files. Most of them mean nothing to me, but some are familiar — Justin Bazini, Daniel and Luca Wood, Vicky Wedge. World leaders. Men and women who owned newspapers and TV stations. Heads of major companies.

One name in particular keeps cropping up. *Dowling*. It's linked with everyone of substance who played a crucial part in the downfall of the human race. The sinister and secretive Dowling seems to have been everywhere at once, pulling strings, manipulating anyone who might be of benefit to his foul cause, setting mankind up for its greatest fall. He got balls rolling, pulled in the main instigators of the unholy assault, organised and distributed funds to anyone who could help him.

Dowling involved Justin Bazini and the rest of the Board. It was Dowling who flew across the world, meeting presidents, generals and religious gurus, asking for their support, demanding it, extracting it.

Dowling who organised the early experiments, who decided the schedule, who set the date.

I never thought one man could wield so much power, so cunningly, so wickedly, so destructively. Or that such a man could keep beneath the radar, unknown to the masses, hidden by his underlings even while he swept across the globe like an undead tsunami.

If these files had surfaced before the zombie uprising, they would have provided all the proof needed to blow Dowling's cover, to expose him to the world for the foul-hearted fiend that he was. But I'm not sure it would have made any real difference. He had so much support from those at the highest levels that I think he could have shrugged off the controversy and pushed ahead regardless. Who could have stopped him when the people loyal to him controlled such massive swathes of government, the military, the media, the major religions?

I know now why Burke's last word was *Dowling*. These files would have tipped any sane person over the edge. I was wrong to assume that my old teacher had run into Mr Dowling and that his brain had been messed with by the clown. It simply went into overload when he read these papers and absorbed so much crushing information all at once.

I also realise that when I held Burke in my arms, and he croaked the word with his last living breath, I misunderstood his intentions. He was trying to warn me, yes, but of a far greater danger than the one I imagined.

I thought I knew the name of my greatest enemy, but I only had it half right. These folders have shown me that the architect of humanity's downfall wasn't my husband, Mr Albrecht Dowling, lunatic clown and all-round psycho killer.

It was his brother . . .

TWELVE

Dr Oystein Dowling.

THIRTEEN

I sit hunched over the folders, staring at the words, slowly flicking through the pages now. I feel sick, numb, betrayed.

There was only one person in this world that I believed in. One constant in my life that I clung to. No matter what else happened, I was sure I could put my faith in Dr Oystein, that he would always stand by those who had pledged themselves to his noble cause, that he – maybe he alone among all the adults I'd ever known – was truly good.

How could I have been so wrong? How could he have fooled so many of us for all this time?

I must be mistaken. The folders have to be crammed with lies. The doc can't be the bad guy. He *can't*. Nobody that caring and loving could be evil at his core. A vicious criminal mastermind couldn't maintain a warm, considerate front, not for that long, not so artfully.

I need to ignore the files, the overwhelming evidence they present, the horrible documented neatness of it all. Look for flaws, discrepancies, forgeries. This is probably the work of Mr Dowling's mutants, or Owl Man, or the Board, someone who wants to turn Dr Oystein's supporters against him. I have to mull this over and proceed cautiously, not make any rash decisions until I've spoken with . . .

'B?'

. . . Dr Oystein in the flesh.

I look up and he's there. Standing before me, beaming, eyes filled with hope, love and concern.

'I was so worried you wouldn't be here,' he cries, striding forward, extending his arms wide to hug me.

'I was angry with the twins. One of them should have stayed with you. I had a sick feeling in my stomach all the way here. I was sure Mr Dowling's men would find you and take you from us again. I think I broke some records as I was racing across from Bow. I didn't know I could run so . . .'

He draws to a halt, taking in my wounds, my sliced-to-ribbons face, my ruined torso, the crown of nails hammered into my head, the endless array of cuts, gouges and scars, the bloodsoaked bandages. I've gone through all sorts of torments since the doc last saw me. He shakes his head, horrified.

'Oh, B,' he whispers. 'What have they done to you?'

I stare at him blankly and say nothing.

'Was this the work of Dan-Dan or Mr Dowling?' Dr Oystein thunders. 'I know that Daniel Wood is dead, so there is nothing I can do about that foul specimen, but if the clown did this to you, I will make him pay. Who hurt you, B?'

I stare at him blankly and say nothing.

Dr Oystein waits for me to respond. When I don't, he licks his lips and glances at the zombies in the room with us, making sure they don't pose a threat. Then he croaks, 'The vial . . . Mr Dowling's sample of Schlesinger-10 . . . is it too much to hope that you might have . . . ?'

I stare at him blankly and say nothing.

Dr Oystein grimaces. 'I'm sorry. That can wait. It was insensitive of me to ask. Maybe the thought never even crossed your mind. We must tend to your injuries. I brought many of your fellow Angels with me. They are waiting outside. We will transport you to our new base as carefully as we can. You'll need to rest in a Groove Tube for a long time. Then I will stitch you together and find replacements for the pieces that have been cut away. I won't lie — you'll never be quite the same again. But I can do more for you than you might imagine.'

I stare at him blankly and say nothing.

'But first . . .' the doc says brightly and produces a syringe. 'This is a concentrated solution of the liquid that we use in the Groove Tubes. It will act like a shot of adrenalin, restore some of your strength and ease the worst of the pain.'

As numb as I am, I know I need that pick-me-up, so I break my silence and mumble, 'That sounds good.'

Dr Oystein crouches next to me and takes my right arm. I observe mutely as he tenderly sticks the tip of the needle into a vein and softly pushes down on the plunger. After pumping maybe a fifth of the liquid into my arm, he removes the needle and inserts it into my left arm, then my legs, one after the other.

'Our blood does not flow swiftly,' he says as he works. 'With others, I would inject it into their heart, and it would be slowly pumped around the body, but obviously that is not an option in your case.' He smiles briefly, then injects the last of the mixture into my neck. 'You should start to notice the effects in a matter of minutes, as your body begins to absorb the solution. You will enjoy only a few hours of relief before your energy ebbs again, but that should be more than enough time for our purposes. I have brought another couple of syringes, just in case, but I do not think we will need them.'

Dr Oystein takes hold of my hand with both of his and squeezes gingerly. 'I've been so worried about you, B. I was distraught when I learnt that you had sneaked out, that Rage had betrayed us, that you had been taken prisoner. If I could have done anything to rescue you, believe me, I would have. But my hands were tied. I had to simply wait and hope and pray.'

I stare at the *good doctor* and fight the urge to curl my upper lip. I tell myself again that I shouldn't jump to conclusions, that there could be more to this than what the folders imply. I have to give him a chance to defend himself. I don't want to accuse him, only to look like an ungrateful fool when he blows the accusations out of the water.

As my flesh tingles and vitality returns to my limbs, I try to think of a subtle way to broach the taboo topic. I don't find one, but I do recall my initial meeting with the doc, and that provides me with my opening line.

'You said that Oystein was your first name.'

His eyes crinkle. 'Pardon?'

'That first day we met, when you were showing me round County Hall, you jokingly said that you'd almost forgotten what your surname was.'

Dr Oystein chuckles. 'You have a good memory.'

'You never did tell me,' I press.

'It's not important,' he says lightly.

'I think it is,' I contradict him. 'Let's play a game.'

'What sort of a game?' he asks, letting go of my hand and staring at me with a quizzical expression, half-smiling, half-concerned, not sure where I'm going with this.

'Let's call it the Rumpelstiltskin game.' I grin humourlessly. 'That was one of my favourite stories when I was a kid, especially the bit where the girl has three chances to guess his name.'

'We do not have time for this, B,' he mutters, and I can tell by the way his expression changes that he knows I've rumbled him. The dark, spiteful look that flashes across his face is all the confirmation I need that the folders are telling the terrible truth. But I carry on anyway, not wanting to believe the worst until I hear him admit it.

'Oh, there's always time for a good game,' I say grimly. 'Let me think ... is your name ... Oystein Smith?'

When Dr Oystein is silent, I pull a long face and answer for him. 'No. So is it ... Oystein Jones?'

Again he's silent, and again I answer on his behalf. 'No. Last chance. Could it possibly be Oystein ...' I start to make a drawn-out D sound, but he cuts me short.

'... *Dowling*,' he says quietly. 'Yes, B, you are correct. I am Oystein Dowling, and Albrecht is my estranged brother.'

I moan wretchedly. I didn't think it would be this easy, that he'd admit his guilt so swiftly. In a way I wish it had been harder. If he'd tried to deny the accusation, I could have gone on believing for a while that it might not be true.

Dr Oystein lowers his gaze. I expect him to attack me or to start offering up excuses, but he only looks around sadly at the folders, taking note of them for the first time.

'I assume you found out through these,' he says with a sigh. 'Nobody was meant to keep a record of what we were doing. I often stressed the need to leave no paper trail. But people cannot escape their nature. I guessed that some would disobey my orders, in case they needed the documents to blackmail me or point the finger of blame solely in my direction. Humans are so predictable.'

He picks up one of the folders and studies the pages, tutting softly. 'I suppose Billy Burke tracked these down. That explains why he tried to kill me. I couldn't be sure, the day he came after me. I hoped that my brother had put him up to it, but Billy didn't strike me as a madman when he stormed into County Hall, just somebody who was very angry. I should have retraced his steps and destroyed the incriminating evidence, but I would have had to investigate by myself — it was not a task I could have set one of my Angels. If I was wrong, and he *had* fallen foul of Albrecht, I didn't want to walk into a trap and end up in my brother's clutches. So I turned a blind eye to the event and hoped it would not come back to haunt me. That was a foolish mistake. I have not made many of those over the decades.'

'Is it true?' I hiss. 'Did you do ... *this*?' I wave a hand at the folders.

Dr Oystein nods slowly. 'Yes.'

I want to hit him with my most barbed insult, but there isn't a curse strong enough to convey what I'm feeling. And if I scream, the Angels outside will rush to his rescue. So I don't bother with words. Instead I hurl myself at the century-old zombie and haul him to the ground.

We roll across the floor and I scrape his face. A couple of fingerbones dig deeply into his left cheek, scarring him.

He doesn't react.

I land on top of the doc and punch wildly, pummelling his stomach, his chest, his face.

He doesn't react.

I grab his head and bang it down hard on the floor. If I had all my strength, I'd smash his skull open and end this clash immediately, but, as things stand, I can only hope to scramble his brains inside their protective covering.

He doesn't react.

I wrap my hands round his throat and throttle him, knowing I can't kill him that way, but wanting to hurt him, to make him cry out, to see pain and fear in his eyes.

He only stares at me miserably.

'Say something, you bastard,' I groan, shaking his shoulders.

He spits blood from his lips and croaks, 'I cannot.'

'Tell me why you did it.'

'Not here,' he says. 'Not now.'

'I'll kill you,' I growl.

'No one will blame you if you do,' he replies calmly. 'Not once you show them the evidence against me. They will probably hail you as a hero.'

'You destroyed the world,' I cry.

'Yes,' he says and his face crumples. I don't see any of the things in his expression that I expected, such as joy, pride, malice. Only misery and grief.

I let go of the defenceless doctor and push myself away.

'B . . .' he says, sitting up.

Before he can say anything else, I put all of my returning energy into my right foot and kick the side of his head as hard as I can. He slumps sideways, not unconscious, but stunned. It will take him a few minutes to recover.

I bend over the gasping doctor and rifle through his pockets. I find the pair of syringes that he mentioned and relieve him of them. I think about stabbing them through his eyes, one for each eyeball. If I stuck them through the sockets and deep into his brain, I could finish him off.

But how can I kill this man who has done so much for me? He rescued me when I was at my lowest. He took me in and showered me with love. He was like my father, only better. I owe so much to Dr Oystein, more than I ever owed to anyone. He guided me, taught me how to put my darker ways behind me, helped me become who I am. If I'm furious and contemptuous now, it's only because he told me to

expect more of people. I hate him so savagely only because I love him so dearly.

It's not for the likes of me to pass judgement on a man like Oystein Dowling. So I take the only option open to a desperate creature in my bewildering predicament. I leave the doc moaning and writhing on the floor. I hurry to the stairs, clutching the syringes tightly. And I run.

FOURTEEN

I wouldn't have made it to the top of the first set of stairs several minutes ago, but juiced up with Dr Oystein's concoction, the steps no longer present a major problem. I lurch up them, growing in strength all the time. I'm still in bad shape, and I sting and ache all over, but coming off the back of my recent lows, I feel like I've been given bionic implants.

I make it to the roof and pause to assess my options. I can hear the Angels out front, murmuring softly, calmly, with no idea yet what has happened inside.

I race along the roof and climb down a drainpipe into the yard at the rear of the building. I hurry across, let myself out of the yard and jog down a long road, then start zigzagging my way south-east, hoping to lose myself in the maze of streets.

I didn't think I'd be fleeing for my life again this soon, or that I'd be running from Dr Oystein and his Angels. Amazing how the world can turn on its head so suddenly.

I silently curse myself as I run, for not killing Dr Oystein. It was crazy, letting him live. But I know I'd do the same thing if the chance presented itself again. I love him too much to take his life, even after hearing his most heinous confession.

There's also the crazy hope that there was a good reason for what he did. If I'd heard him out, maybe he could have explained it in a way that made sense.

At the same time, that possibility was why I ran. I was afraid he'd convince me that the slaughter of billions could be justified. I know in my (missing) heart of hearts that there can be no excuse for unleashing the zombie virus, but I think he could have provided one regardless. If he had, and I'd bought his story, I might have forgiven him and carried on working with him.

That would have made me as guilty as he is, and I don't want such a stain on my conscience. Some things in this world should be unacceptable no matter what. Sometimes you shouldn't allow people to grey your vision, to make you stop seeing an atrocity in simple black and white terms.

I remember discussing the Holocaust once with Vinyl and a few of my other mates. I told them my dad had said that the number of victims had been vastly exaggerated, that certain groups wanted to make it seem worse than it was, in order to squeeze extra sympathy out of people worldwide. According to him, only a few hundred thousand Jews had been killed, and in concentration camps, not death camps.

Vinyl stood up at that point and snarled at me. He said he had a simple policy when it came to Holocaust deniers. As soon as they started spouting crap, no matter how reasonable it might sound, he walked away, because some things were never worth listening to. And off he stormed. The rest of the gang followed him or went home, heads low and unusually silent, leaving me to glower at the pavement by myself.

I felt very small that day, angry at Vinyl for humiliating me, but also angry at myself for being willing to believe my dad's distortions of the truth. I knew Vinyl was right, and I know he'd act the same way today if he was still here. He's not, but I can at least do his memory justice. It's not much of a comfort, but I'm sure my old friend would be proud of me if he could see the way I cut Dr Oystein off before he could start spinning his seductive lies.

Yeah — but he'd have been prouder if I'd rammed the steel-tipped end of one of Timothy's paintbrushes through the old goat's skull!

I allow myself a wry chuckle at the thought of bringing Dr Oystein down with such an unlikely weapon. Then I hear the sound of footsteps and I fall silent and listen.

The runners aren't making a lot of noise, but in a city of the dead it's just about impossible to mask the echoes of dozens of feet slapping on the pavement. There are lots of people tearing after me, and I'm certain they're Angels.

Master Zhang will be furious when he finds out how his students reacted. They should have come in smaller gangs and padded softly, sacrificing speed for stealth. I wouldn't want to be in their shoes when they report back to him. Unless of course they capture me. Nobody will care then.

I'm surrounded by houses. Many of their doors are ajar, either left that way by their owners when they fled, or forced open by zombies. I slip into one of the deserted shells, not touching the door, and position myself in the shadows of a room with a window overlooking the street.

The Angels come tearing past. They're in a pack, hunting like dogs. No sign of Dr Oystein, which makes me suspect he's led another group in a different direction. I figure they probably split into four teams, maybe more. They'll want to cover the main routes out, north, south, east and west.

If I'm right about that, their apparent clumsiness

begins to make sense. As bright as I feel, it's only relative to how poorly I felt before. I'm nowhere near as strong or fast as the other Angels. I only have a few minutes' head start on them, so they know I can't have gone far.

My colleagues aren't racing after me in a disorganised rush, as I first assumed. They're running to get ahead of me. When they're sure they've outpaced me, they'll stop, break into smaller groups and track back, examining every street and alley, every building and house.

There won't be enough of them to cast an impenetrable net across the area, but it will be hard to slip through. Clever sods. Strangely, I'm proud of them, pleased to see they haven't lost their heads when the heat is on, even though I'm the scared rabbit that they're hunting.

I've got two choices. I can find somewhere to hide and hope they don't root me out. Or I can try to sneak through the closing web of Angels undetected.

In a city like London, there are more hiding places than a person could count. There's no way the Angels can check everywhere. It wouldn't be a sign of cowardice if I laid low, just a mark of common sense.

But then I'd be like Anne Frank and others who hid during the Second World War. It worked for some of them and they evaded capture, but it must have been horrible, holed up in the gloom, knowing they were doomed if their enemies found them, flinching at every unexpected sound or movement. I don't want to saddle myself with the fear, the tension, the paranoia every time a rat scuttles past.

Also, my newly regained strength won't last. I feel reasonably fine now, but I won't in a few hours. Even if I inject myself with the other syringes, I'll only buy myself half a day, maybe a day at best, and I'm sure the Angels won't abandon the search that swiftly.

Flight is my preferred option. If I'm going down, I want to go down fighting, in the open, not cornered and helpless. It would make sense to slip into the sewers and try to lose them in the dark, but I've spent enough time underground. I'm sick of the tunnels and bunkers. I belong up here, in the land of day and night.

I step out of the shadows, a devil-may-care smirk on my face. I stride back through the doorway and out on to the road. I continue the way I was headed. And inside my head I issue a challenge to the big, bad world — 'Come get me, suckers!'

FIFTEEN

I cross Whitechapel Road and continue south-east, looking to hit Limehouse at some point. I did think about reversing direction and heading west, since Dr Oystein's new base is situated in the East End, but they might anticipate that. In their position I'd focus the majority of my forces north and west, the areas where a fugitive would be most likely to run.

Of course, they might have anticipated my anticipation and sought to second-guess me, but I'm not going to drive myself crazy by thinking like that!

I go slower than previously, listening, watching. Cunning will serve me better than speed right now. It's a game of cat and mouse, and since I can't outrun my hunters, I need to outsmart them.

I keep to the inner sides of paths, ready to duck into a building if I catch sight of any Angels. But the streets seem to be deserted. The zombies are resting in the shade, while the living abandoned their claim to the pavements long ago.

I spot movement ahead and throw myself through the broken window of a coffee shop. I look for weapons, but there's not much that will be of any use in a fight. In the end I grab a couple of long spoons. If I can't stab, at least I can gouge.

I position myself close to the door, figuring it will be better to strike as they enter, rather than wait in the back for them to come find me. I hold the spoons loosely, biding my time.

There are shuffling sounds outside and I prepare for battle.

Then a zombie stumbles into view and I relax. It's an old woman, green moss growing thickly across her collarbone, where she was bitten when alive. One of her eyes has been torn out. It looks like a relatively fresh wound. She's moaning softly. I can tell she's hungry, in even more pain than most of her kind. Desperate for the brains which will ease her suffering. Willing to brave the discomfort of the daylight world in order to search for scraps that the faster, sharper zombies might have missed during their night manoeuvres.

The zombie turns her eye on me, determines I'm no good to her and pushes on. I feel sorry for the old biddy, but there are millions more in her lousy position, and there's nothing I can do for her.

Then I have an idea and step out after the woman. I thought when I first saw her that she was an Angel. So there's a good chance that if any Angels catch sight of her, they might think she's me. Some of them will probably have stationed themselves in houses, keeping watch, hoping I'll pass by. The zombie might lure them out, or distract others who are on the street. I can use her as a diversion, follow at a distance, duck for cover if I spy anyone darting towards her.

I wait for the pitiful old lady to get a good way ahead of me, then trail after her, matching her sluggish pace, letting her act as my unwitting decoy. As long as she keeps going in the direction that I want, she'll be a good addition to the team.

We inch along, an unlikely partnership. I cover as many angles as I can, looking behind, left, right, my head snapping around like an agitated bird's.

A shadow passes overhead. I look up immediately but there's nothing there. Lots of small clouds are scattered across the sky. I guess the shadow must have been one of those, though it seemed to scud by too swiftly for a cloud.

The old woman pauses to pick through some over-turned bins in the middle of the road. I don't know what she expects to find. I'm annoyed by the delay, and think about cutting her loose and going my own way again. I keep glancing up, unsettled, not con-vinced that the shadow was a cloud, but telling myself that I'm just being paranoid. This is the reason

I didn't want to hole up. When your brain gets spooked, you start to see trouble everywhere.

Eventually the zombie abandons the bins and pads onwards. She rounds a corner. I shuffle after her, but before I can turn into the new road, someone leaps from the roof of the building and lands in front of me. I'm still holding the spoons from the coffee shop. I raise them defensively ... then lower them when the guy straightens up and faces me.

He's a good-looking teenage boy with dark hair and fashionable, trendy clothes. He's usually a cheerful sort, but his face is clouded with anger now.

'You are in so much trouble,' Carl Clay growls.

'Tell me about it,' I sniff. 'Are the others with you?'

'Of course.' He whistles, and Shane and Ashtat step out of a hairdresser's. The ginger Shane is in his customary tracksuit, tacky gold chains dangling from his neck. Ashtat is wearing a blue robe and a golden headscarf.

I thought my injuries would provoke a reaction, but Dr Oystein must have told them about my sorry

state because they barely spare my horror show of a body a second glance. They both look as pissed off as Carl, too angry to bother with sympathy or concern.

'It's like a class reunion,' I chuckle as my ex-room-mates from County Hall gather in front of me. 'A pity Jakob is missing. That would have made a full set.'

'Rage too,' Shane says.

'Nah,' I grunt. 'He was never one of us. Not really.'

The Angels eyeball me and I return their gaze silently.

'You must be out of your mind,' Carl finally hisses. 'Assaulting the doc? Taking off like a bat out of hell?'

I shrug. 'What did he tell you?'

'That you were upset,' Ashtat says icily. 'He said you were not yourself, that it was imperative we find you, but we should not hurt you unless we had absolutely no other option. We were not to approach you, but to send for him, so that he could confront you personally.'

'Sly old Dr Oystein,' I sneer. 'He wanted me all to himself. No surprise there.'

'What are you talking about?' Carl frowns.

I shake my head. 'It doesn't matter. Have you sent word to him?'

'No,' Ashtat says. 'We want you to come freely. We do not know why you struck Dr Oystein, but if you surrender willingly, we are sure this can be worked out.'

'We were over the moon when we found out you were alive,' Shane says. 'We don't want to lose you now.'

'We're sure it's not your fault,' Carl snorts. 'Mr Dowling must have messed with your mind when he was slicing up your body. The doc will be able to help you get your head back in order. He'll clear up everything if you give him a chance.'

'You don't have a clue,' I huff. 'I've been through hell since you last saw me, but that had nothing to do with why I attacked Dr Oystein. He's not what he seems. He's been playing us for fools. He –'

'It's all right,' Carl says soothingly. 'He told us you'd say stuff like this. The clown has turned you against us, so you think we're the enemy. That's OK. The doc will set your brain straight again. But you have to come with us, B. We can take you by force if necessary, but we'd rather not.'

'You need to trust us,' Ashtat says. 'We are your friends. We care about you. We want to help.'

'I know you do,' I mutter sadly. 'But you don't have all the facts. There's nothing wrong with my brain. I unearthed a secret while I was waiting for the doc. It changed everything. Give me five minutes and I can explain it all. Then I'll show you the proof, if the doc hasn't already disposed of it. Five minutes isn't too much to ask, is it, after all that we've been through together?'

The three Angels look at one another, considering my request.

'No,' Ashtat sighs. 'There is nothing to discuss. We will not let you level false accusations against Dr Oystein.'

'You don't know what you're saying, B,' Carl says sympathetically. 'You'd be wasting your time, trying to make us believe your lies.'

'Give it up,' Shane grunts. 'There are four of us to one of you. You don't stand a chance.'

157

'You never were good at maths, numbnuts,' I sneer. 'There's only three of you.'

'Four,' someone with an American accent says softly behind me.

I whirl and spot a ghost from my past.

'*Barnes?*' I cry.

The ex-soldier and one-time hunter of zombies looks grim. He's dressed in dark clothes, a rifle strapped across his back, a handgun in a holster dangling from his left hip. There are more streaks of grey in his black hair than I remember. He's still got a bullet jammed behind his right ear. He's pointing a taser at me and is packing a couple of spares in his other hand.

'Hello again, Becky Smith,' Barnes says solemnly.

'What the hell are *you* doing here?' I gasp, wondering if I'm imagining things in my addled state.

'I've been back in London a while now,' Barnes says quietly. 'I turned up at County Hall not long after you'd left, to offer my services to Dr Oystein.'

'Barnes was the one who led us to you,' Shane says admiringly. 'He guessed your most likely route and

brought us with him to intercept you. He told us how to search for you.'

'You haven't lost your old hunting skills,' I snarl, fixing my gaze on the taser, getting ready to throw myself out of the way of the dart-like electrodes as soon as he fires.

'Look me in the eye, B,' Barnes says softly.

'Get stuffed,' I jeer, moving sideways, preparing a battle plan, trying to keep sight of the Angels while watching Barnes's trigger finger.

'B,' Barnes says more firmly. 'I want to see your eyes.'

Something in his voice makes me look up. We lock gazes and he stares at me with a calm, hard expression. I'd been brandishing the spoons, hoping to ward off any incoming blows, but now I let them drop, knowing I can't fend off a warrior of Barnes's stature with a couple of useless bits of cutlery. The game is truly up.

'Go on then, you bastard,' I croak bitterly. 'Knock me out and take me to your precious new master, the same way you served me up to your old bosses.'

'Dr Oystein isn't the same as Justin Bazini or the Wood brothers,' Barnes says.

'You're right there,' I agree. 'He's worse.'

'See what they've done to her?' Carl says miserably.

'Yes,' Barnes murmurs, not breaking our connection, looking into me almost as deeply as Mr Dowling used to. 'I see.'

Then his jaw sets and he takes a step back. Before I can react, he raises the taser, aims swiftly but carefully and fires.

SIXTEEN

The barbed electrodes shoot through the air and find their target. The taser buzzes as electricity shoots through it and I wince in anticipation of my muscles spasming, my limbs stiffening involuntarily, before I collapse and thrash about like a dying snake.

But to my surprise I don't fall. Not a single muscle twitches. After a confused moment, I realise that's because Barnes didn't shoot me.

He shot Shane.

As Carl and Ashtat gawp, Barnes calmly takes the

second of his three tasers and shoots Carl, who falls next to Shane.

Ashtat recovers her senses and turns to run, but Barnes is too quick, even for a revitalised zombie. The electrodes catch her between the shoulder blades and she goes down with a strangled cry.

Barnes leaves the electrodes attached to the tasers and doesn't cut the power. He lays the hand units down, checks to make sure that each is functioning, then sets his sights on me.

'That's the same sort of taser I used when I captured you outside Hamleys,' he says. 'One blast should knock each of them out of action for a good while, long enough for us to get away. But I don't believe in taking chances. I'll leave them running. They won't cause any permanent damage.'

'I don't get it,' I say warily. 'Why are you doing this if you're Dr Oystein's man?'

'I'm nobody's man except my own,' he replies stiffly. 'I quit taking orders the day I severed my ties with the Board. I worked for Oystein because I believed in him.'

'And now?' I ask.

He shrugs. 'I believe in you more. You're the reason I came back. I never forgot how you fought every day to spare the lives of those children on the *Belfast*, even though you had no ties to them. I left London to try to save my son, but I couldn't shake the feeling that I should have stayed to fight with you. When I got done with my other business, I reckoned I might put my dubious talents to their best use if I threw in my lot with you. So here I am.'

I stare at the tall, serious-looking man, wondering if this is a trick.

'How can I trust you?' I growl.

He smiles wearily. 'If you tell me not to come with you, I'll let you go. I found you once, so I could probably find you again, but I won't come looking if you ask me not to.'

'And Dr Oystein?' I press. 'He won't be impressed when he finds out you've betrayed him.'

Barnes snorts. 'I knew there was something wrong when he came out of the Brewery without you. He fed his Angels a load of crap, claimed Mr Dowling had done something to your mind, that you were out of control. But that's not the story the twins told when they reported back. According to them, you were in bad shape physically but fine mentally.'

Barnes looks around impatiently. 'We don't have time for this conversation, not here in the open. I don't know what's happened between you and Dr Oystein, but I can smell a rat. I doubt you would have fled without good cause, and I don't think he'd have sent his troops after you if he wasn't desperate to get you back. Desperate men worry me. I have little faith in them.'

'You're crazy,' I laugh.

Barnes doesn't crack a smile. 'I feel I owe you for all that you suffered on the *Belfast*, since I was the one who delivered you to Dan-Dan and the others. I'll help you if you want, or release you if that's what you'd prefer. Just give me the nod.'

I think it over quickly and decide to gamble on his support. 'Come on then,' I grunt, and off I set, no longer alone, and no longer as vulnerable as I was. I don't want to jinx myself, but, with Barnes by my side, I just might make it out of this trap. There's hope for the B yet!

SEVENTEEN

Barnes takes the lead and I'm happy to follow. I like waiving the responsibility. I've carried the can long enough. Let somebody else do the planning and worrying for a while. It makes a nice change.

The ex-soldier sets a slow pace, not much faster than the speed I was going before I fell in behind the one-eyed zombie.

'Aren't you worried we might run into other Angels?' I ask.

'Hush,' he says. 'The Angels don't bother me but zombies do. If they see or hear us talking, they might investigate, and I don't want to have to flee from a pack of brain-munchers.'

I'd forgotten that the undead were a threat to the likes of Barnes. I'm full of questions, but I keep my mouth shut, respecting the silence. Now that I study him, I see that he's not just walking slowly, but swinging his arms and rolling his head, the way many zombies do. He's mimicking the movements of a revived, to divert the interest of any undead observers who might be wondering about the couple of figures swanning around in the sunshine. He also covers his head with his arms every so often, as if the rays are paining him.

I haven't a clue what time it is, but, to judge by the setting sun, we don't have much daylight left to play with. I think of mentioning that to Barnes, but I'm sure he's even more aware of it than I am. The streets of London are deadly for the living at night.

Barnes leads me south into Wapping. I don't think that's a good idea. The streets are narrow here, the buildings pressing in tightly above them. Easy to fall foul of a flash zombie attack and get pinned down.

But he seems to know what he's doing and he starts to pick up the pace, negotiating the streets as if he's familiar with them.

We don't run into any Angels. I'm glad of that. As far as I can see, Barnes is out of tasers, leaving him only with his guns. I'd rather not harm any of my old allies. They weren't part of Dr Oystein's conspiracy. They don't know what the doc is really like.

As the sun starts to set over the city, freeing the undead to come out in their hordes, we arrive at a pub called the Prospect of Whitby. The windows have been boarded over and the door is locked. To my surprise, Barnes produces a key.

As the door opens and we slip inside, I whisper, 'That wasn't a skeleton key.'

'No,' Barnes says, closing the door behind him and flicking on a light. 'This was one of my bases in the old days, when I was running with Coley. We shored up several places like this around the city, so we could stay in them at night when we needed to. We'll be safe here.'

Barnes pushes through the pub, switching on another few lights. He goes all the way to the back door, opens it and steps out on to a balcony overlooking the river to check something. He's smiling when he returns.

'The last time I was here, I left a boat tied up outside. It's still there. We have that as backup if we need to make a quick getaway. It's not much of a craft, but it'll get us safely out of here if zombies attack from the front.'

'You think of everything,' I chuckle.

'No,' he sighs. 'But I try to.'

Barnes fetches a bottle of beer from a fridge, opens it and finishes off half with his first gulp.

'Damn, that was good,' he gasps, setting it down. 'I'd almost forgotten what beer was like, even when it's well past its sell-by date. I'd offer you one, but I know it would run clean through you.'

'I'm too young for alcohol anyway,' I smirk.

'Sure,' he laughs. 'Like you never sank a sneaky beer or two in your misspent youth.'

We smile at one another and I take a seat close to

him, but not so close that I might accidentally scratch him if he was to stumble.

My smile fades as I remember something. 'You mentioned Coley a minute ago . . .'

Barnes grins. 'Poor old Coley. I felt bad for turning on him the way I did, tying him up before I rescued you from the Board. I went back and set him free. He was mad as hell – would have tried to kill me, except he figured I'd take him in a fair fight – but he swallowed his pride and actually asked to come with me. He knew he stood a better chance of getting out of London if he had someone to watch his back. But I could never have trusted him. I made my excuses and left. Haven't heard anything about him since. I guess that's the last I'll ever see or hear of him.'

'Well, it's definitely the last you'll *see* of him,' I sniff and proceed to tell Barnes about how Coley teamed up with Dan-Dan again, and how his master killed him when the zombies overran Battersea Power Station.

Barnes is grim-faced when I finish. 'The fool,' he snaps. 'He deserved what he got, siding with a monster like that. We didn't know about the children when we signed up to work for the Board. But to understand what Dan-Dan was truly like, and to go back for more ...' He spits with disgust. Then his expression softens. 'Still, we were a team for a long time. I hoped he'd fare better than that.'

'At least it was quick,' I note.

'Yeah,' Barnes says glumly. 'We should all be so lucky.'

He sips his beer and I give him a few moments of silent reflection. Then I clear my throat as tactfully as I can. 'What about your son?'

'Stuart,' Barnes says softly, staring at the label on the bottle.

'Did you find him?'

Barnes doesn't answer. His son was the reason he caught me and handed me over to the Board. They'd granted the boy sanctuary on a zombie-free island which their people were managing. The child was safe as long as his father cooperated with Bazini and his cronies. But then Barnes betrayed them and led the Angels to my rescue.

Barnes finishes the beer and gets another. I say nothing, determined not to ask any more questions, not wanting to upset him. But after a while he looks up and volunteers the information.

'It took me longer to get to the island than I imagined. A lot of roads to the coast were blocked. I had to work my way around them. I ran into scores of zombies. But I got there in the end. I kept going. For Stuart.'

The ex-soldier's fingers tighten on the bottle and I know what's coming next.

'Bazini or one of his team had radioed ahead. Told the people on the island what I'd done, and issued new instructions. I found Stuart's remains. They left him hanging over the harbour. He was still there when I reached the island. Well, whatever the crows hadn't bothered with.'

Barnes falls silent again, his gaze distant, a world of pain in his expression.

'Did you kill them?' I ask softly.

He shakes his head slowly. 'I don't blame them. They were following orders. I knew what the rules were when I signed up to the deal. I broke them, so it was my fault, nobody else's. There are always consequences when you agree a deal with evil men. After what I did on the *Belfast*...' Barnes sighs. 'Anyway, I cut down what was left of Stuart, buried him, then got the hell out of there, unseen and unheard.'

'Do you regret it?' I ask quietly. 'Telling Dr Oystein about me. Leading him to the *Belfast*. Breaking your contract with the Board. Would you do it differently if you could go back in time?'

Barnes grunts. 'No. If you're a damn fool once, you'll be a damn fool twice. What they were doing on the *Belfast* was wrong. I'd always known they were a crooked bunch, but I was able to turn a blind eye to their shortcomings — I'm no saint myself, so I didn't feel any right to take the moral high ground. But when I realised the full extent of their vileness, of what Daniel Wood was doing to those children . . .

'There are some things in this life that you can't stand for,' he says, which is similar to what I'd been telling myself earlier in the day. 'I loved Stuart more than anything else in this world, but sometimes you have to make a sacrifice for the greater good. I'm not sure if Stuart would have understood that. It wasn't really something I understood myself until I saw those children on the *Belfast*. I wish I could have one last conversation with my boy, to explain.'

'I'm sorry,' I croak.

Barnes sniffs, waves my apology away, then has another gulp of his beer and tries to forget the awful loss that his decency has cost him.

EIGHTEEN

It wouldn't have surprised me if Barnes had carried on drinking, to wash away the memories and sleep the dreamless sleep of a drunkard. But he stops after the second bottle. I assume that he wants to be alert if we have to move out in a hurry.

'You hungry?' Barnes asks, pulling some dried goods out of a chest.

'That stuff's no good to me,' I snort.

'I know,' he says, 'but I have brains too. I keep them in a freezer out back. I had a look when I was checking the boat. The power to the freezer went a while ago, but I think the meat's still fresh enough to be of use.'

'What are you doing with brains?' I frown.

'Coley and I kept a supply. We used them to bait zombies and lure them into traps.'

'Very humane,' I mutter, my expression hardening.

Barnes shrugs. 'I make no apologies for being a hunter. I don't regret killing brain-dead zombies. They're savage abominations and this world is well rid of them. I'm sorry for what I did to you, but that's as far as my regrets extend. The dead should stay dead and, if they don't, the living have every right to put them down.'

I shift uncomfortably. I want to argue the point with him, but how can I when just a few hours ago I was plotting to unleash a virus that would wipe out every zombie on the planet? Barnes cut down dozens or hundreds of reviveds in his time. If I'd been successful, I'd have eliminated billions.

'Get the damn brains,' I huff.

Barnes grins and fetches me a slice of chilled headcheese. It's not the most appealing chunk of brain

I've ever been faced with – a light mould has spread across it since it defrosted – but it hasn't totally dried out, so it should still provide me with the nutrients I need. As I take it from him, he settles back and his grin spreads. 'I can't wait to see this.'

'What are you talking about?' I snap.

'I want to see how a stomachless zombie eats.'

I stare at Barnes, then at the hole in my middle. 'Hell, I hadn't thought about that.'

'You haven't eaten in a while?' he asks.

'Not since most of my stomach was ripped away.' I think about it, then take an explorative bite. I work it down my throat, but once it clears my chest, the chunk simply drops into the pit where my bowels used to be.

'Plop!' Barnes deadpans.

'I'm glad you're enjoying this so much,' I scowl. 'If I can't eat, I can't extract the nutrients that I need to keep my brain ticking over. I'll relapse and become a revived again.'

'There's no fear of that,' Barnes says. 'I've seen zombies in worse shape than you chowing down and getting whatever it is that they need from the brains. Go with your instincts and see where they lead you.'

I stare at the chunk of brain in my hand and try to tune out my thoughts, to focus on the food and let my natural reactions take over. It's easier than I thought it would be, and a minute later I find myself mashing the brain up in my mouth, working it into a paste. Then I spit the paste into my hands and scrape it around the walls of my stomach, covering as much of the cavity as I can with the grisly goo.

'Fascinating,' Barnes purrs.

'You don't have to gawp,' I growl. 'I know how disgusting this is.'

'No,' he says. 'This is better than prime-time TV. Is it doing the job? Do you think you'll be able to sustain yourself?'

'Yeah. I can already feel myself absorbing the richness of the meat. I'll scrape off the gunk soon, so as not to attract insects, but it's pretty much the same as when I ate before. Except now I don't have to puke the brains back up, so in a way it's even better.'

'You'll set a trend,' Barnes laughs and tucks into his

own food, which looks a hell of a lot more appetising than mine.

Barnes carefully washes his plate when he's finished and throws the remains of my mashed-up meal into the Thames, so that the scent doesn't attract any passing zombies. I join him on the balcony and stare out across the river. Night has settled over the city and I can hear the moans and cries of its undead population as the reviveds take to the streets in search of the ever-diminishing supplies of grey matter.

Brains must be hard to come by now. The vast majority of zombies are surely in agony. I think the noise will worsen over the coming months, until maybe it's one solid, twenty-four-hour-long scream, every single day of the week for the next few thousand years.

'I don't know why they stay,' Barnes says quietly. 'Surely they'd be better off in the countryside, where they might find the odd wild animal to feast on.'

'There are still lots of animals here,' I tell him. 'We can smell their brains. But they're fast, and they hide, and they're able to adapt. The reviveds are slower to change. Maybe they never properly will. But as long as the scent of brains lingers, zombies will prowl the streets. They don't have the sense to move on.'

'It's a hell of a world,' Barnes says bitterly, then heads back inside. I stay on the balcony a few minutes longer, listening to the howls of my brethren, wishing I could cry or, failing that, cast aside my consciousness and join them. But since I can't and won't, I turn my back on the tortured shrieks of the city's damned souls and follow Barnes into the pub, where we can shut the door on the night and act for a while as if all is as it was when the world was the domain of the living.

NINETEEN

'So tell me about Dr Oystein,' Barnes says.

'You mean Dr Dowling,' I correct him.

When Barnes raises an eyebrow, I explain about the folders, how Dr Oystein's surname is Dowling, how the doc confirmed that he's Mr Dowling's brother, that he was the main figure behind the release of the zombie virus.

I don't think Barnes is often left speechless, but he can't say anything for a long time after I finish. He stares at me as if I have two heads. That doesn't surprise me. I find it as bizarre as he does.

'I don't understand,' he finally mumbles. 'Oystein has saved so many people. All of his time is dedicated to trying to eradicate the undead and hand control back to the living.'

'That's what he says,' I snort. 'But I think it's a sham. He's been looking to get his hands on Schlesinger-10. We thought –'

'What's Schlesinger-10?' Barnes interrupts.

'A virus he concocted. It can wipe out every living person, leaving the zombies free to rule the world alone. Owl Man stole it from him before he could put it to use, and gave it to Mr Dowling.'

'Hold on,' Barnes stops me. 'I'm getting confused. Owl Man and Mr Dowling are the villains here, aren't they?'

'Well, they're definitely not the heroes,' I laugh, then shake my head. 'It's complicated. Mr Dowling loves chaos, so he wants to keep things as they are, the undead pitted against the living, him in the middle, relishing the bloodshed. He's not good or bad as we see it, just totally bonkers. But at least he wasn't planning to wipe out humanity. That much we know for sure, since he could have uncorked his vial of Schlesinger-10 at any time.'

'OK,' Barnes nods. 'Not an ally, but not a direct foe either.'

'Oh, he's definitely a foe,' I disagree. 'Just not a foe who wants to kill all of the living.'

'What about Owl Man?' Barnes asks.

I purse my lips. 'He's more difficult to pin down. I've no idea what his motives are. He was involved in the spread of the zombie virus – his name was all over the files – but at the same time he didn't release the sample of Schlesinger-10 when it was in his possession, so I guess he's not trying to annihilate every living human either.'

Barnes frowns. 'So you're saying Oystein is the only one who wants to use this virus to kill us all?'

'It looks that way,' I shrug.

'Then why didn't he simply recreate it after the first batch had been stolen?' Barnes asks.

I make a small humming noise as I think about that. 'Maybe he couldn't. Mr Dowling was his partner before they fell out with one another, and Owl

Man was their assistant. Maybe one of those two was instrumental in figuring out the formula, and the doc couldn't replicate it without their help. He was able to make Clements-13, but that was no good to him.'

'Clements-13?' Barnes echoes.

I tell him about the other virus, the one that can put the undead back in their coffins where they belong.

'Dr Oystein told us it was a stand-off. He said that if he released Clements-13, killing all the zombies, Mr Dowling would release his sample of Schlesinger-10, dooming all of the humans in return. Now, based on everything I learnt today, I guess it must have been the other way round, that Dr Oystein was the one who wanted to unleash Schlesinger-10 and eradicate humanity. That's why he was so eager to retrieve Mr Dowling's sample, not to neutralise it, but to use it.'

I feel a lump in my throat as I give words to my thoughts. It hurts me, condemning Dr Oystein out loud like this, but it's the truth, so how can I turn away from it? I've been fighting a war against evil ever since I linked up with the Angels, but all this time the enemy has been in our midst, trying to trick us into helping him get his hands on the ultimate weapon.

'What about this Clements-13 you mentioned?' Barnes asks, distracting me from my melancholy. 'Does Owl Man or the clown have that too?'

I scratch one of my metallic ears thoughtfully, finding it hard to focus. 'I'm not sure. I don't think they'd be bothered about it. I mean, even if Dr Oystein released Schlesinger-10, they wouldn't use Clements-13 against him, because it would kill them too.'

'So nobody's going to use the Clements-13 virus?' Barnes presses.

'I doubt it. Maybe the doc doesn't even have a sample any more. Hell, maybe he never developed it in the first place. That might have been a bluff, to make us believe that he was on the side of the living.'

Barnes thinks about that for a long time. I leave him to it. My head is hurting. I wasn't made for mental acrobatics of this kind.

'Of course, this is all pure conjecture,' he finally says, not content to let it lie. 'Any chance the doc might have been framed, or that you misunderstood him, that he really does want to help the living?'

'Possibly,' I sniff. 'Bloody unlikely, I'd say, but I didn't hear him out. I didn't dare. I was afraid he might convert me if I gave him a chance.'

'Wise girl,' Barnes chuckles, then pulls a confused face. 'This is messed up. I've dealt with double-crosses and intrigue for most of my life, but nothing on this scale.'

'It's simpler than it seems,' I tell him. 'Schlesinger-10 is the key. Dr Oystein used the zombie gene to bring the world to its knees. Now he's looking to get hold of the thing he needs to crush the last of the living completely.'

'Unless you've got the wrong end of the stick,' Barnes says.

'Unless I've got the wrong end of the stick,' I admit.

'But where do *you* come into the equation?' Barnes asks. 'Why does the doc want you so badly? It can't be just because you know about his true role in this. He would have told his Angels to kill you if that was the case. But he gave them orders to bring you back alive.'

I start to tell Barnes about my marriage to Mr Dowling, but before I get to the part where I pinpointed the location of the vial of Schlesinger-10 and smuggled it out in the lining of my stomach, I have a nasty thought and I pause.

What if Barnes is here on Dr Oystein's business?

I'm pretty sure he's on the level. I think he really did help me because he likes me. But I've been taken for a ride by an apparent Good Samaritan before. Maybe it's a trick. Maybe Dr Oystein told him to stage a betrayal, to con me into trusting him, so that I'd tell him what I did with the stolen vial — and I'm sure the doc knows that I did steal it, because that's the only reason why Mr Dowling would have invaded County Hall. This could be part of a cunning plan.

'B?' Barnes asks when I fall silent.

I stare at the ex-soldier, wanting to trust him, but

wary after what happened with the last person I had faith in. Should I take him into my confidence or keep him at arm's length?

'You know what?' I mutter in the end. 'All this talking has made me hungry. I didn't realise how famished I was. Could I have more brains, please?'

Barnes's eyes narrow. He can tell I'm suspicious. For a dangerous moment I think he's going to attack me. But then he smiles and says, 'What the hell. I might have a few more biscuits myself while we're at it. We deserve a treat after what we've been through.'

He goes to fetch us some grub, leaving me to gaze at the back of his head and wonder miserably — friend or foe? Have I found sanctuary here or walked into a trap of Dr Oystein's making?

TWENTY

I don't need the extra helping of brains, but go through the motions, still mulling things over, trying to work out my next move. Whatever I decide, it will pay to keep Barnes sweet. As a zombie, I can't sleep. If I get the sense that something's rotten, all I have to do is play along, wait for him to nod off, then slip away while he's snoozing.

Barnes brews a mug of coffee and sips from it after finishing his biscuits. He's obviously not a dunker.

'The offer still stands, you know,' he murmurs over the rim of his mug.

'What offer?' I ask.

'You can leave any time.' He nods towards the back door. 'The boat's yours if you want it. You can sail off down the river by yourself, go wherever your path leads you. I won't try to stop you. You're not beholden to me.'

'I wouldn't get very far on my own,' I mutter.

'Bullshit,' Barnes snorts. 'You'd get further than just about anyone else I know, even though half of you has been snipped away. I'll give you all the brains that are stored here, and you have the syringes you took from Oystein to help top up your energy levels.'

'How do you know about those?' I snap.

'The doc told us. The twins had said you were dead on your feet — no pun intended. Oystein informed us that that was no longer the case. Warned us to be cautious.'

I chew at my lower lip, studying Barnes's face for the least hint of a lie. He must see the worry in my gaze because he smiles lazily and extends his hands.

'Tie me up if you want. Then make your get-away.'

I stare at his hands and frown uncertainly.

'Damn it, B, I can't make my position any clearer,' he growls, losing patience. 'It's obvious you don't trust me, and I understand why you feel that way. But I'm not going to have you scrutinising my every word and gesture. Accept me as an ally or cut me off and go your own way. But don't hang around and doubt me. I deserve better than that.'

'Do you?' I ask bluntly.

'I risked my life for you,' he snarls.

I shrug. 'I didn't ask you to.'

His nostrils flare and he points an angry finger at me. Then he squints, takes a second to think about it and sighs.

'You're right. You didn't. And I'm doing what I said I wouldn't — trying to persuade you to stay. Make up your own mind. I'm not going to try to charm you.'

Barnes gets up, roots through a pile of books on a shelf, chooses one and sits again, opening it quietly and carefully, as if in a library.

I watch him reading for a couple of minutes. It's

some old spy novel. I think my dad had a copy of it at home.

'Tell me I can trust you,' I say softly.

'No.' Barnes lowers the book slightly. 'But I'll tell you this, even though I'm probably wasting my breath. I wasn't sure if life was worth living after I buried Stuart. I didn't sob or howl at the moon. That's not the sort of guy I am. But I sat in a quiet corner of a deserted church when I got back to the mainland, a can of beer in one hand, a gun in the other. And I thought long and hard about if I could be bothered carrying on.'

Barnes goes back to reading the book, but his hands are trembling now – not much, but a little – and I'm sure he's not concentrating on the words.

'Why did you choose to continue?' I ask, remembering my own decision to end it all as I trudged away from County Hall, certain that everything was lost.

'Believe it or not, I thought about *you*,' Barnes replies. 'It wasn't intentional. I was sitting there, remembering Stuart, mourning all that I'd lost, figuring there was no reason for me to go on fighting and struggling now that he was gone.

'Then I found myself thinking about brave Becky Smith, how she didn't give in when she was a prisoner, how she fought the good fight, how she'd have surely been killed if I hadn't interceded and led the Angels to her rescue. I knew she was the sort who was going to get into trouble again, and I had a niggling feeling she might need my help further down the line.

'I spent a long time drinking that beer,' Barnes says, his voice a bare croak. 'Trying to decide if helping you mattered to me that much. In the end it was something I'd said to Stuart when I first left him on the island that swung it. He didn't want to stay. He didn't care that he was safe there. He cried and begged me to take him with me, said he couldn't stand it if I abandoned him and never returned.

'I told him that if he truly loved me, he wasn't to think that way. If I fell to the forces of darkness during my travels, I said the best way he could honour my memory was by living his life to the full.

I told him to look for a father figure on the island, find someone who could take my place. He said he could never do that. I told him that if he didn't, it would mean he'd never loved me as much as he claimed.'

Barnes is still holding the book, but he's looking at the ceiling now. There are no tears in his eyes, but I think he's probably as close to them as he has ever been, or is ever likely to be.

'You're my replacement for Stuart,' Barnes says hoarsely. 'I lost my son, the only person on this dirtball of a planet that I loved, and I've replaced him with a foster daughter, to do for him what I hope he would have done for me.

'I lived because of you, B,' he finishes softly. 'If I can save you, I'll keep the ghost of my son alive a while longer. When I pass from this world, I'll take the last loving memory of Stuart with me, and I want to put that off for as long as I can. Protecting you gives me the willpower to endure the pain and heartache, to limp on when it would be so much easier to just stop.'

Barnes clears his throat and scowls. 'Believe me if you want, or believe I'm full of crap if you prefer. I don't give a damn. Just let me read my book in peace.'

And, having said that, he returns his gaze to the novel and acts as if I'm not there, leaving me free to choose.

TWENTY
-ONE

'My dad died in Battersea Power Station,' I murmur after a while.

Barnes squints. 'What was he doing there?'

'He was in the Ku Klux Klan. One of their shining lights.'

The ex-soldier blinks. 'I didn't know you were of racist stock.'

'Oh yeah. The very worst. I used to be that way inclined myself once, eager to please my daddy.'

'And now?' Barnes asks.

I smirk. 'These days I figure, live and let live.'

Barnes laughs out loud, then smothers it with a palm, not wanting to attract the attention of any sharp-eared zombies who might be lurking nearby.

'I'd like to have a father I could love and respect,' I tell him when the fit of laughter passes.

'B . . .' he says, his voice crackling with deep emotion.

'But since there's no one like that around, I suppose you'll do,' I add.

He shoots me the finger. 'You're not what I expected from a daughter either,' he chuckles.

'What?' I act shocked. 'I'm not Daddy's little princess?'

'Daddy's little monster more like,' he smirks, then lays his book aside. 'Does this mean you don't think I'm angling to betray you?'

'I'm giving you the benefit of the doubt,' I mutter. 'For now.'

'I feel privileged,' Barnes says with a straight face. 'In that case what's our next move? Since you didn't kill Oystein when you had the chance, I'm guessing you aren't interested in revenge.'

'Nah. What would killing him achieve? If he was just a nasty sod like Dan-Dan, I might go after him. But someone who devotes his life to bringing down an entire species is a nutter of a different order. If I thought he still posed a threat, I'd have to act, but I'm pretty sure he can't do any more harm.'

'You're not concerned that he'll get hold of Mr Dowling's vial of Schlesinger-10?' Barnes asks.

'No,' I grunt, not telling him any more than that. I do trust him, but, even so, there's no point being a silly bugger about it and sharing more than I need to.

'So what next?' he asks again.

'Do you think you can fix me?' I ask, pointing a finger at my shredded midriff.

Barnes leans over and studies the damage. Looks at the stumps of my shorn-off ribs, the places where Mr Dowling screwed in attachments which the babies later ripped away.

'How do you talk without lungs?' he asks.

'Mr Dowling inserted a pump in my throat before he removed them,' I explain.

Barnes unwraps some of the bandages that are

holding me together and surveys the rest of the damage, the holes in my arms and legs, my lacerated cheeks. His face saddens as he stares.

'Less of the pity,' I huff. 'I don't need it.'

'They really did a number on you,' he notes.

'Yeah, well, we can't do anything about that. I took the abuse and I'm still taking it. No point moping. Focus on my stomach. That'll be a major drawback if we can't patch it up.'

'There's not a lot I can do,' Barnes says. 'I'll wrap some fresh bandages round you — proper bandages, not these useless strips of cloth.'

'Hey,' I scowl, 'they were all I had.'

'And I guess they did the job,' he admits, 'but they're not the long-term solution. Tomorrow we'll screw in bolts to give you the rough shape of a ribcage, then cover them with a plastic sheet or a strip of leather. It needs to be something more durable than bandages, but easy to remove at the same time, because you'll have to go on eating like you did tonight, mashing up brains and smearing them in.'

'Mr Dowling was able to build an artificial digestive system for me,' I sniff.

'Bully for him,' Barnes retorts. 'Go back to him if you were that impressed with his handiwork.'

'What, and abandon my daddy?' I grin. 'OK. First we'll sort out my stomach. Can you fetch what you need in the morning?'

'Not a problem,' Barnes says. 'I can have you ready to go before midday.'

'Great. I'll need some new clothes too — my dress is a wreck. Once I'm good for the road, we'll get the hell out of this place. I'm sick of London and the lunatics who control it. I want to get as far away as I can from Dr Oystein, Mr Dowling and the rest.'

'Do you have your sights set on anywhere in particular?' Barnes asks.

'New Kirkham,' I reply instantly.

'I know that place,' Barnes nods. 'Coley and I swung through there a few times. Decent people for the most part, but some bad eggs in among the mix.'

'It's changed since you last saw it. The racists made a play for power but failed. They were all hanged for mutiny. One of my friends helps run the town now. He'll give us shelter. We can draw up a more concrete plan, then set off into the wide blue yonder.'

'Sounds good to me.' Barnes stretches and yawns. 'Now, if you don't mind, I'm going to rid you of the rest of those old rags, wrap you up good and tight with clean bandages, do a bit more reading, then turn in for the night. You can keep watch. I might as well make use of you now that you're here.'

'I'm not a guard dog,' I growl.

'Of course not,' he says sweetly. 'You're far uglier and way more vicious than any common mongrel.'

'That's right,' I huff, 'laugh it up. We'll see if you're so clever when I bring you your slippers in the morning and *accidentally* scratch your ankles when I'm helping you put them on.'

Barnes laughs and says, 'That's my girl.'

'If only,' I whisper to myself, remembering my real father and thinking what a pity it is that we don't get to choose who our parents are. 'If only.'

TWENTY
-TWO

A few hours later, Barnes is snoring lightly. He fell asleep almost as soon as he turned in. He'd told me that would be the case. He also said he's a light sleeper and would probably wake up if there were unusual noises, but, even so, not to hesitate to disturb him if I thought there was a suggestion of trouble brewing.

Barnes sleeps in a sleeping bag on the bar, out of the way of any rats or insects. His guns rest close by, as well as a collection of knives. He didn't take off his boots or clothes, saying he liked to be able to hit the ground running. When I joked about his smell, he said it was no laughing matter. Zombies have an easier time sniffing out a clean human than a filthy one.

I tried reading to pass the time, but I wasn't able to concentrate. I kept thinking about Dr Oystein, what he's done to the world, why he hates the living so much, if there's even the slightest chance I might be wrong about him. Brooding about the past. Worrying about the future.

I want to go sit on the balcony, but I'd wake Barnes if I got up, even if I tried to tiptoe. He said not to worry, that he snaps awake several times most nights, but I don't want to be a disruptive guest. He came to my rescue today, when I was sure all was lost, so I want to repay him as best I can.

Am I foolish to hope that things might work out? Will Dr Oystein anticipate my return to New Kirkham and send Angels there ahead of me? Should we take a random route out of the city, avoiding any places that either of us has ventured to before? And afterwards, if we escape, where do I want to wind up?

An island free of zombies? If so, what would I do about getting hold of fresh brains?

Even if we could go somewhere by ourselves, where there was a ready supply of brains, surely Barnes would pine for human company. I'm limited in what I can give him. Conversation, yes, but we can't touch. No hugs or high fives. I can never give him a bunk-up if he needs it. No contact sports. I'd even have to be wary playing a game of cards, in case I got excited, reached for a card at the same time as him and scratched him by accident.

Maybe I'll let Barnes go his own way once he's escorted me to safety. Perhaps I could settle in a town or city in another country, where I could raid the morgues for years to come, lonely but safe. Leave Barnes to live with others of his kind. Pop by for a visit every so often, to let him see that I'm OK and cheer myself up.

I don't contemplate suicide. That's off the agenda. I only toyed with that idea when I thought I was alone in the world. Now that I have someone who cares about me, who might need my help just as I need his, I'm giving no thought to my ultimate end. The grave can't have me as long as I have the interests of a friend to consider.

I smile warmly in the dim light of the old pub, feeling like I've turned a corner, despite everything else that has happened.

And that's when I hear a sniffing sound outside.

TWENTY
-THREE

I'm too wise to the ways of the world to dismiss the noise. As soon as I hear it, I jerk bolt upright and hiss, 'Barnes!'

He wakes instantly, sits up, grabs a gun and looks at me questioningly. I point to my ears, then at the front door.

Barnes slips out of the sleeping bag, slides off the bar counter and stares at the door. We stand where we are, listening. I can't hear anything now, but I know the sound was real.

Barnes slowly, softly crosses to my side and whispers, 'What was it?'

'I'm not sure,' I reply quietly. 'Something snuffling. Maybe a zombie with a blocked nose, but it didn't sound like one.'

'An animal?' Barnes asks.

'Possibly. But big if it was. Not a rat. More like a . . .'

I stop, suddenly realising what the noise reminded me of. A dog. There are still dogs in London. They usually lie low at night, only coming out when the sun is up. I suppose some of them break that rule, creeping forth when it's dark, to forage for food if they feel like they can outwit or outrun the undead. Maybe the noise came from one of them, a hungry mutt on the prowl.

But there's another type of dog. A unique specimen. One which has followed me before.

As a wave of panic rises within me, I turn to Barnes and start to tell him that we have to get out of here immediately, that we must not take any risks.

Before I can say a word, the lock in the door clicks as someone fiddles with it.

'The balcony,' Barnes says calmly, raising his rifle and pointing it at the front door.

'I think I know who it is,' I mutter, grabbing a knife from the counter.

'Not a friend, I assume?' he says bleakly.

'No.'

The door starts to open. Barnes pulls the trigger and the top half of the door explodes into splinters. There's an angry howling noise. Some of the splinters must have caught the dog.

'Run!' Barnes grunts, slowly backing up, ready to fire again if he catches sight of anyone.

I hurry to the rear door, throw it open and step on to the balcony. I look around to make sure there's nobody waiting to pounce, then move to the edge of the platform to jump down into the boat.

It isn't there.

I stare at the space where the boat should be, then out across the river. I spot it bobbing up and down in the middle of the Thames. There's a large, familiar figure on board. He waves heartily to me.

'Hi, Becky,' Rage hollers. 'Fancy bumping into you here.'

Barnes hears and looks back at me. 'Are we screwed?'

'Pretty much,' I growl. 'Any other way out?'

'The roof. There's a ladder on the balcony. Set it up and –'

'Becky,' a man on the street shouts. 'This does not have to end badly. We can cut a deal.'

'Who's that?' Barnes asks.

'Owl Man,' I wince. 'The dog is Sakarias, his pet hound. It must have tracked my scent. I never anticipated that. I should have. It's not the first time the thing has hunted me.'

'No point blaming yourself now,' Barnes says coolly. 'The boat?'

'Rage has taken it.'

'Is there anybody with him?'

'Not that I can see.'

'Do you think they're likely to have brought backup?' he presses.

'I've no idea. But hopefully not. I think I'd have heard more noises if the mutants were with them.'

Barnes sniffs. 'If it's just them, then it's three

against two if you count the dog. Those are the sort of odds I like.'

'Becky?' Owl Man calls again. 'You won't gain anything if you try to run. I only want to chat. We'll let your friend walk away unharmed if you come out without a fight.'

'I'm going nowhere,' Barnes replies before I can answer. Then he whispers to me, 'Scram. I'll stall them as long as I can.'

'No,' I groan. 'I won't leave you.'

'You don't have a choice,' he says.

'Of course I do,' I argue. 'I can stay and fight.'

Owl Man pokes the front door open and it swings inwards. Barnes fires again, but there's no one there. Light from the moon spills into the bar.

'Please, Becky,' Owl Man says. 'I won't hurt you. If you value your partner's life, lay down your weapons and tell him to depart.'

I look at Barnes and grimace. 'He's offering you a way out. I think he'll honour his pledge if I surrender.'

'I won't abandon you,' Barnes says stiffly.

'But we're trapped.'

'No we're not. Get up on that roof and hotfoot it out of here like I told you.'

'And I told you I won't leave you.'

Barnes glowers at me, then shrugs. 'In that case let's hit the street and take the fight to them.'

'Becky?' Owl Man asks.

'Give me a moment,' I call sweetly, then move ahead of Barnes.

'What are you doing?' he snaps.

'The dog could rip your head off with one bite. And it can move quicker than anything you've ever seen. If you go first, Sakarias will attack.'

'What makes you think it won't attack you?' Barnes asks.

'They want me alive. I'll act as a shield, confuse them, buy you a few seconds. You can use that time to blow their stinking heads off.'

Barnes grins grimly. 'I like it. OK, you lead, I'll follow. Just don't forget we're a team. I'll be watching your back all the way. Don't feel that you have to cut me loose to protect me. We escape or go down together. Agreed?'

221

'You're the boss, *Dad*,' I smile.

Barnes returns the smile, then slips up close behind me. We start to advance.

'Oh, Becky,' Owl Man sighs, sensing rebellion in the air. 'If you had trusted me, we could have avoided this unpleasantness.'

'I do trust you,' I shout cheerfully. 'I'm coming out now. I've laid down my weapons, honest I have, and so has Barnes.'

I'm nearly at the door. I get a firmer grip on my knife.

'You think that you can fool me, but you're only making a fool of yourself,' Owl Man says wearily. Then he clicks his tongue. 'Here, Sakarias. I want you by my side. Good dog.' He raises his voice. 'One last chance, Becky. Turn yourself over to us. Let Barnes walk away from this.'

'Ignore them,' Barnes growls in my ear. 'They can't hurt us, not if we work as a team.'

'Here we come, Owly,' I chirp. 'Time for tea and crumpets.'

'Silly girl,' Owl Man murmurs. 'Will you never

learn?' He clears his throat and his voice changes, becomes deeper, more commanding. 'I want you to do something for me, Becky.'

'Yeah?' I sneer. 'What's that?'

'Kill Barnes.'

I start to laugh, but before the sound can form, I find myself turning swiftly. Barnes isn't expecting it. He backs up and stumbles. My hand snakes out towards him. He probably thinks I'm trying to steady him. But he's wrong. Because it's the hand holding the knife. And, as Barnes stares at me with shock and disbelief, I drive it through the side of his head, all the way up to the hilt.

TWENTY -FOUR

I let go of the knife and stare with horror at Barnes as he blinks dumbly, lips moving mutely. He reaches for the handle of the knife, to pull it out, but his strength deserts him and he slumps. I catch him as he falls and lower him to the floor, moaning over him as he starts to shake.

It doesn't take long for Barnes to die. His eyelids soon stop twitching and his mouth goes still. I set his head down and turn it sideways. I'd like to pull out the knife and kill myself with it, but Barnes looks peaceful. I don't want to make a mess and disturb his body.

I push myself to my feet and glance at the doorway. Owl Man is standing there, Sakarias by his side. The dog is panting. Owl Man looks grim.

I throw myself at the bar, scrabbling for another couple of knives, one for the creep in the pinstriped suit, the other for myself.

'Stop,' Owl Man snaps, and I come to a trembling standstill.

'Hands by your sides,' he commands, and my treacherous limbs obey.

Owl Man and his dog move into the bar. Sakarias trots over to Barnes and sniffs his face, making sure he's dead. Owl Man stays focused on me.

'You forgot that I could bend you to my will, didn't you?' he asks softly.

'I'll kill you,' I snarl.

'I will not give you the chance,' he says, then sighs. 'I am sorry about the soldier. He might have proved a useful ally. You should have come out when I gave you the opportunity.'

I try forcing my hands to rise, my feet to move, so that I can launch myself at Owl Man and rip his face to pieces. But I'm a statue. He has complete control over me.

'The end is nigh, Becky,' Owl Man says, coming closer, touching my left cheek tenderly. 'Our suffering is almost over. Once the final hand has been played, we can start afresh. It will be the beginning of a whole new era. Life will be easier for us then.'

'I'll kill you,' I snarl again.

Owl Man tuts. 'I could try to convince you to see things our way, but I know you would not heed my protestations. It is time for action, not words. However, before we push on, there's someone who has more faith in words than I do, and he would like an audience with you.'

I stare questioningly at Owl Man. In response, he points towards the door, and I realise someone is with him. A third figure steps into the room, a slight, neatly dressed man with greying hair and a kindly face which has been recently scratched and bruised. I have to do a double take, because I never would have expected to see him in the company of Owl Man, but there can be no mistake — it's Dr Oystein.

'You!' I cry. 'What the hell are *you* doing here?' I nod at his large-eyed companion. 'With *him*?'

'Why shouldn't I be with Tom White?' Dr Oystein replies calmly, referring to Owl Man by his original name. 'He is, after all, my nephew.'

As I stare at the doc incredulously, mind reeling at the revelation which has been so casually tossed my way, he takes a seat, calmly runs a hand through his hair and regards me solemnly. 'Becky Smith,' he says heavily, 'it is time for you and I to have a little talk.'

To be concluded ...

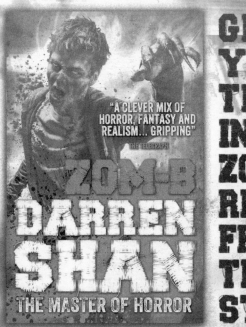